"Pull over!"

Sissy exclaimed as they were nearing the fudge shop and the dock. Elijah did so, pulling into a conveniently vacated parking space. "You want chocolate this badly?"

"Not chocolate! We have to do this." She jumped out of the car, pulling Whiteout after her by his leash.

Elijah followed her across the street to the fudge shop, and a moment later he saw her approach the jukebox. Then he heard the opening strains from outside.

She rushed out, laughing, beautiful and giddy, kicking off her white high-heeled sandals and moving into his arms and singing with the words. He sang them back to her, sang of only and always and the greatest blessing of his life.

Sissy said, "We have to hear it three times."

Elijah threw back his head, laughing, and Whiteout jumped up on them both, kissing Sissy's face. She was too interested in Elijah, in the love and excitement she felt from him, to admonish the dog. She looked into Elijah's brown eyes and murmured softly, "Down, boy."

Dear Reader,

This is Harlequin's 60th Anniversary, a celebration for Harlequin authors and readers. I'm both, and have been since I was very young, as a lot of the books around our house were Harlequin romances first read by my grandmother and/or sisters. These books swept me away to exotic settings, caught me up in fascinating conflicts.

Daily, I'm thankful that I write for Harlequin Books, grateful for the lovely people associated with this company, faces I'm delighted to see at romance writers' conferences, voices I know only over the phone, talented professionals who work hard to put together books readers will love.

Even more than that, I'm grateful for you, my readers. For me, you are at the center of the Harlequin experience. Nothing makes my day like a note on Facebook or MySpace from a reader who says she enjoyed one of my books—or even, incredible to me, that I'm her favorite author. As I write these books, you are with me. I know you're going to read what I write, and I want it to move you, to entertain you, to help you forget your cares.

I hope *Here to Stay* accomplishes this for you, that you enjoy this love story about a hero and heroine truly destined for each other and how, over decades, they overcome past hurts to embrace the deep, rich love to which they have committed.

Wishing you all good things always.

Sincerely,

Margot Early

Here to Stay
Margot Early

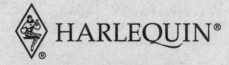

TORONTO • NEW YORK • LONDON
AMSTERDAM • PARIS • SYDNEY • HAMBURG
STOCKHOLM • ATHENS • TOKYO • MILAN • MADRID
PRAGUE • WARSAW • BUDAPEST • AUCKLAND

Recycling programs
for this product may
not exist in your area.

ISBN-13: 978-0-373-78334-2

HERE TO STAY

www.eHarlequin.com

Printed in U.S.A.

ABOUT THE AUTHOR

Margot Early has written stories since she was twelve years old. She has sold 3,600,000 books with Harlequin; her work has been translated into nine languages and sold in sixteen countries. Ms. Early lives high in Colorado's San Juan Mountains with two German shepherds and several other pets, including snakes and tarantulas. She enjoys the outdoors, dance and spinning dog hair.

Books by Margot Early

HARLEQUIN SUPERROMANCE

766—WHO'S AFRAID OF THE MISTLETOE?
802—YOU WERE ON MY MIND*
855—TALKING ABOUT MY BABY*
878—THERE IS A SEASON*
912—FOREVER AND A BABY*
1333—HOW TO GET MARRIED
1357—A FAMILY RESEMBLANCE
1376—WHERE WE WERE BORN
1401—BECAUSE OF OUR CHILD
1436—GOOD WITH CHILDREN
1546—THE THINGS WE DO FOR LOVE

*The Midwives

HARLEQUIN AMERICAN ROMANCE

1229—HOLDING THE BABY

To Oak and Carrie Smith of Oak Ridge German
Shepherd Dogs with thanks for your love,
friendship and beautiful dogs

CHAPTER ONE

My uncle's dogs taught me of the species'
profound attachment to humans, a loyalty
seemingly indestructible, even through inhu-
manity.
 —*Dog Brethren,* Elijah Workman, 1977

Echo Springs, Missouri
July 2, 1956

TWELVE-YEAR-OLD Elijah Workman pedaled his
bike through the saunalike heat, away from his
father's shop. Up Ghost Hill and beneath the
green trees, hurrying to the Atherton place to feed
their dogs, then over to his uncle Silas's place to
get paid for the two days Elijah had fed his dogs.
His uncle had taken two dogs with him on his
recent fishing trip to Arkansas, but had left Elijah
in charge of two pit bull puppies and four adults.

Elijah was caring for only a handful of the
Atherton family's canines; like his uncle, they

had many. The Athertons had taken several of their German shepherds with them to Kansas City for a dog show, so Elijah was earning money caring for those they'd left behind.

Elijah loved all dogs, and though he'd never been allowed to have one of his own—his parents said they were too expensive—he'd figured out ways to spend plenty of time with the animals. What did he care about the American Kennel Club or the snobbishness of the Athertons or the other snobbishness of his own uncle? Elijah didn't rub shoulders with the Athertons in normal circumstances. They knew that he wasn't intimidated by their animals and he would never mistreat them. They knew this because dog-sitting was Elijah's business, and he had been running this business since he was eight years old. He had references. His family was poor, and Elijah contributed to the household with the money he earned, though his mother made him save half of it in case he wanted to go to college some day.

Elijah finally reached the white fence surrounding the Athertons' eighty-acre spread, their trees, stables and kennels. He turned in their groomed driveway, pedaling over the gravel. The German shepherds began barking.

They were handsome, Elijah silently acknowledged as he rode up to the kennel fence. "Hi,

Ruby," he greeted the Athertons' champion conformation bitch, who was in season and had been
left at home. Four years ago, he had brought his
uncle's pit bull bitch Ella to show-and-tell on the
same day Sissy Atherton had brought Ruby to the
same event.

It hadn't been pretty, and afterward Sissy's
father had threatened Elijah's uncle. That was the
last time Elijah had taken a dog to school. No
doubt Ruby would have been killed were it not for
the third-grade teacher setting off the fire alarm,
which distracted Ella for a nanosecond, allowing
Elijah to grab her collar and drag her backward.
He hadn't been strong enough—Ella loved to
fight, so he'd done it in a superhuman way. His
father had told him that happened sometimes.
When his father had worked in the quarry, he'd
once hefted a boulder the size of a trash can off
another man. *It's amazing what you can do when
you're scared, son.*

Elijah leaned his bike against the kennel as
Ruby wagged her tail at him, wearing her big
goofy grin. He next greeted the other dogs who
hadn't gone to the dog show, four older shepherds
and a rascally one-year-old named Warren.

Elijah headed for the home's screen porch,
where they stored dog food in big cans.

"You don't need to feed them."

Elijah spun around.

Sissy Atherton, in a pale green sundress, her corn-colored hair in a kinky perm around her long, bony face, sat in the shade on the steps of the big wraparound porch.

"What are you doing here?" Elijah demanded.

"I live here?" she said in that snotty tone that only Sissy Atherton could pull off.

"Where are your folks? Are they back from the dog show?"

"No. But Kennedy and I are here, so you needn't worry about the dogs."

Sissy's older sister, Kennedy, went to an eastern university named Swarthmore. Elijah scanned the area and noticed Kennedy's Thunderbird parked under the big oak tree. He tried to remember everything the Athertons had told him before they'd left for the dog show. "You're supposed to be at camp," he finally said. Some kind of ballet camp.

"It's over. Kennedy picked me up. So you can go home and watch a dogfight or something."

Elijah squinted. "A dogfight?"

"Doesn't your uncle have dogfights?"

Elijah supposed this might be true. He, of course, had never been to one. Dogfights were illegal, and once when he'd asked his father if Uncle Silas was involved with them, his dad had simply said, "That would be against the law."

Which hadn't answered Elijah's question. Uncle Silas said that his dogs were athletes. They played with something called a springpole, and they had a treadmill. Also, they loved to climb trees. Ella was Elijah's favorite, but she'd gone fishing with Uncle Silas this time.

Elijah wasn't sure how to respond to Sissy's accusation. He settled on repeating his father's words. "That would be against the law."

"Not to mention cruel and disgusting," she said, tossing her kinky hair. Elijah's mother thought Sissy was pretty. Elijah thought she was too tall and you couldn't see her eyebrows or eyelashes because they blended in with her face. She was flat-chested. Besides that, she was stuck on herself and thought she knew everything about things she knew nothing about.

For instance, she didn't pay attention to her dogs—not really. She did things with them, he was pretty sure, but he doubted she really paid attention to them, tried to figure out what they were seeing and hearing, what they wanted. And each wanted different things. Ruby, for instance, would rather chase tennis balls than eat. Warren appeared to prefer food to just about anything. And Elijah had a feeling that old King would really like to chase small furry animals, kill them and eat them. Though Elijah wasn't one to trust to feelings. He just saw how King spotted squirrels and watched them through the fence, as though if the fence were gone he would be, too, in a heartbeat.

Elijah said, "I told your folks I would feed the dogs, so I better do that."

"I *said* you don't need to. They're our dogs, after all."

"Who's going to feed them then? Where's Kennedy?"

"Why do you need Kennedy?" Sissy demanded. *God, she thinks she's queen of the realm.* "Because she's an adult. If I'm going to stop feeding the dogs, I need to make that arrangement with her."

The screen door swung open, and Kennedy Atherton stepped out. She wore a white dress, and she was very blond, very voluptuous, and in Elijah's opinion, very beautiful. Not, however, particularly nice. The only Atherton he really liked was Mr. Atherton, who knew interesting things about animals and was always *wondering,* the same way Elijah wondered about things. Mr. Atherton wondered what Ruby was thinking when her huge nose twitched. He wondered if when the German shepherds smelled a scent they also pictured the thing that had made the scent. He wondered what were the thoughts of dogs, and for this Elijah respected him.

Kennedy said, "What is it? Hello."

Elijah could tell she didn't remember his name.

"Mom and Dad had him feeding the dogs, but now we're home so he doesn't have to."

Kennedy gazed at Elijah with a thoughtful frown. "No," she said, "he can keep doing it."

"I can do it," Sissy said.

"I'll explain *later,*" Kennedy hissed to her sister.

"I usually feed them. They're my dogs."

"Let's let this young man do his job and earn his *money,* Sissy."

As he got on with feeding the dogs, Elijah suspected he should feel insulted. But he did want the money.

He looked up from refilling water bowls as Sissy entered the kennel. The German shepherds stood up to greet her. Ruby was in her separate pen, away from the others, where none of the dogs could form a tie with her through the chain link, which Uncle Silas had told him dogs were quite capable of doing.

Sissy said, "My father says everyone knows your uncle matches dogs and that he should go to jail, but no one can catch him."

Elijah didn't like the idea of Uncle Silas going to jail or being perceived as a criminal. "Probably because it's not happening," he told her.

"You think," she said. "It's a blood sport. Dogs get their faces ripped off."

She was certainly an unusual girl, Elijah reflected. He had no doubt she loved Ruby and her family's other dogs, yet she casually mentioned dogs getting mutilated, an image that turned his stomach. "That's sick," he said.

Her expression changed, and Elijah had the feeling he'd passed some kind of test. Sissy had gotten Warren to sit, and she crouched down to pet him. "Warren, you're never going to be a show dog, are you?"

"What are you going to do with him?" Elijah asked. Speaking of inhumane practices, he'd heard someone say the Athertons drowned puppies who weren't of show quality. Elijah believed this no more than he believed the stories about his uncle and dogfights.

"I meant he'll never be a conformation champion," Sissy said. "Dad thinks he could finish, but—well, he's mine anyhow. I'm going to show him in the obedience trials in St. Louis next weekend. Want to see what he can do?"

In spite of himself, Elijah was intrigued. "When I'm done feeding everyone and cleaning up. Yeah," he agreed.

WARREN WAS INATTENTIVE, and Sissy lamented the weeks of separation made necessary by ballet camp. Once on lead, he surged to the end of the leash. As she'd been taught by her mother, she spun around one-hundred-and-eighty degrees, using her whole body to winch the leash tight, and ran in the other direction. Warren seemed to think this was a game and immediately surged to the end of the lead again. Not uttering a word to him, Sissy repeated the process several times until Warren seemed bored. Then she began walking him around the yard through a heeling pattern, alternating slow, regular and fast paces. But Warren sniffed the grass. He was supposed to sit each time she stopped, but apparently had forgotten the fact. Sissy found it mortifying.

On the sidelines outside the ring's low white fence, Elijah Workman watched. Elijah was cute, but he would never look twice at her, Sissy knew, not in the way she'd have liked. He had dark brown hair and brown eyes and was almost as tall as she was, which was unusual. She'd been the tallest person in her class for as long as she could remember. Also, he was one of the brighter boys; the teachers liked all the Workman kids. Poor but hardworking as Kennedy had just pointed out, Elijah probably needed the money he got from taking care of dogs.

Nonetheless, his uncle, Silas Workman, who ran fishing tours out on the Lake of the Ozarks, gave Sissy the creeps. Elijah must be delusional if he thought Silas wouldn't stoop to something criminal, and she believed her father about the dogfighting. Her father hadn't been talking to her, of course. He would never criticize another adult—or another child, for that matter—to her. He'd been talking to her mother, and he hadn't known Sissy was in the next room behind the door or she knew he wouldn't have said any of it. In her family, if you wanted to learn anything interesting, you should be prepared to eavesdrop.

When she finished all the obedience exercises, she told Elijah, "He's usually a little better. I think he's distracted."

"I don't think he knows why you're yanking on the leash. You ought to tell him when he does things right. Tell him he's good. Maybe use some food, too, to get him to walk right beside you. I'd bet he'd do anything for food."

"You can't *talk* in the ring during an exercise. And you definitely can't use food. Besides, I want him to know he has to pay attention to me."

"So tell him he's good."

"Dogs aren't like that," she said as though it was the last word on the matter. "They need to respect you, and coddling them doesn't make that happen." Sissy regarded Warren thoughtfully. "He's handsome, but he has a goofy ear."

Elijah had noticed that one of Warren's ears didn't stay up all the time.

"We had him neutered because Dad didn't want to risk him mating with one of the bitches. Also, so he won't fight. He gets along with everyone."

Elijah had noticed Warren's temperament and admired it. His uncle's dogs, which were certainly of a fighting breed, had to be kept in careful combinations. None of the females could be together and only a couple of the males could be with some of the females. He always had to write down which dogs were friends and which weren't because his uncle had assured him that fights could result in one or both dogs being badly hurt. Which proved Uncle Silas did care about his dogs and which certainly counted against Sissy Atherton's claim that he matched them in pit fights.

Nonetheless, many dogs liked to fight, including some of the Athertons'. Gertrude, the German shepherd bitch who was at the show with them was a hellion. She would fight with any of the other dogs, and Elijah thought she'd rather fight than eat.

Sissy said, "Gertrude might become a champion this weekend. She's in Kansas City. She just needs a major."

A "major," Elijah had picked up, had something to do with conformation titles, which were a complicated business that didn't interest him much. What he had gathered about conformation, however, was that it seemed to produce nice-looking dogs. Of course, Mr. Atherton would preach for ten minutes at a time about foolish judges who picked unsound dogs. He would never breed a dog with any problem he believed to be hereditary, even if it didn't affect the dog's looks. But plenty of breeders did breed unsound dogs, and this made Mr. Atherton angry.

"Agnes is being bred this weekend," Sissy added.

Elijah silently longed for one of the Athertons' German shepherd puppies. Then he shut down the thought—he was not allowed to have one. And now he had to get over to Uncle Silas's and pick up his money.

"WHERE'S ELLA?"

Uncle Silas's champion pit bull Satchmo had bounded up, docked tail wagging, as soon as Elijah entered the yard. Elijah had greeted him and the other dogs as Uncle Silas stepped out onto the steps of the trailer he'd built into a permanent home. He was tall like his brother, Elijah's father, and today he wore a white tank undershirt with his trousers. He lit a cigarette as Elijah joined him, holding it between his thumb and forefinger. His eyes were overly bright, almost wet.

"Where's Ella?" Elijah repeated.

"Gone." His uncle sucked on his cigarette, crouched and rubbed Satchmo.

"Gone where? Did she run off and get lost while you were fishing?"

Uncle Silas seemed to consider the question. "No. She's passed on."

But Ella was a young dog, only five! "Did she get sick?" Elijah asked.

"She was hurt. Had to put her down. That's all."

Elijah could see that his uncle was upset, sad about the death of his dog, so he asked no more. He wondered how Ella had been hurt, and he felt his own eyes getting too warm at the thought that he wouldn't see her again or rub her brindle fur. He missed the wrinkle in her forehead.

He petted Satchmo, then hugged the dog. Satchmo kissed his face.

"Let's see what I owe you, son," his uncle said.

ON THE RIDE HOME, Elijah's stomach bothered him. He was sad about Ella being gone. She was the closest thing he'd ever had to a dog of his own, and if he'd been with her she wouldn't have gotten hurt. He kept wondering *what* had happened, and the wondering was what made his stomach hurt.

As he reached Y Road to head for his house, he

saw a girl on a bicycle approaching, and he recognized the awful blond perm. It was Sissy Atherton.

He didn't want to talk to her, which meant he was either going to have to pedal very slowly or very fast to avoid a conversation. He tried the first method, but at the Stop sign she braked. Seeing him, she waved and waited.

Almost as though she'd been looking for him.

He rode up to her. "Yeah?"

"That's friendly," she said.

"What are you doing?" he asked.

"Just riding around." She was all red. It was pretty hot out.

"Well, I have to get home for dinner," he said.

"Were you at your uncle's?" she asked.

He nodded and started to ride away.

"Well, bye," she said.

HOW OBVIOUS CAN YOU GET, Sissy Atherton? she asked herself as she turned her bicycle, riding toward the gas station on Y2 for a soda. *He probably knows you were hoping to see him.*

She shouldn't have tried to run into him. He hadn't been friendly. *He doesn't like you, Sissy. He's never going to like you.* And now he must think she was chasing him. She would have to come up with a story to explain why she'd been out on Y Road, but she'd already told him she was just riding around. Maybe she'd say she'd let one of the dogs loose and was looking for it and hadn't wanted Elijah to know so her parents wouldn't find out and she wouldn't get into trouble. But that plan could backfire, too, since her parents might hear the story anyway. They'd be mad if she told them she'd lied, but they'd be madder if they thought she'd been careless with the dogs.

She drank her soda at the gas station where Mr. Harrelson's son was working on cars. Mike was seventeen and very good-looking. All the girls thought so.

Sissy finished her drink and pedaled home by the dirt lane between the Harrelsons' land and the Corys' place with its weeds. Her father said Max Cory had taken good care of the property, but he'd died and his son was letting the place go to seed. Sissy thought Vincent Cory was scary, and he kept mean dogs chained in his yard.

So when she saw a doglike shape ahead of her on the dirt lane, she stopped her bike, wondering what to do. If she turned around and rode away, the dog would chase her. If she rode past, the dog might attack her.

She wondered if she could turn around without the dog noticing her, but before she could move, it started toward her. There was something wrong with it, though, with the way it was moving, and its face looked wrong. It also seemed thin.

She held still, then stooped to pick up some rocks. She ordinarily wouldn't consider hurting a dog, but Vincent Cory's dogs were mean.

But this one's face was all black.

No, that was dried blood and flies.

ELIJAH'S FATHER'S PICKUP TRUCK finally pulled into the gas station. Sissy had tried to call Kennedy first, but the line was busy, probably because Kennedy was talking to her boyfriend.

When Mr. Harrelson saw the trembling, skeletally thin dog Sissy had been holding by its collar with one hand, he'd said, "Honey, can't no one do nothing for her."

The animal was a reddish pit bull bitch, Sissy thought, and she'd believed at first it must be one of Vincent Cory's. But Sissy had never seen it before, and she was too afraid to go to the Cory house and ask. Nor could she possibly walk away from the dog. She had no idea what could do such a thing to an animal.

Sissy wasn't going to let Mr. Harrelson shoot the dog, which he had expressed willingness to do; Sissy couldn't stand it if that happened. The pit bull was missing an ear, and Sissy couldn't find her features in her face. It was the worst thing

Sissy had ever seen, but surely a vet could help her.

So she'd called Elijah, reasoning it was okay because this time she *wasn't* chasing him; she was just concerned about the injured pit bull. Also, his job was looking after dogs, so maybe he would know whose bitch it was.

And now the green pickup truck was here, the bed full of tools and lengths of pipe and other stuff as usual. Elijah's father was a pipe-fitter and welder.

Elijah climbed out of the passenger side, and his father got out from behind the wheel. Mr. Workman was tall and broad-shouldered, and he wasn't creepy like Elijah's uncle.

Elijah saw Sissy but ignored her as he ran to the bitch and crouched down to look at the animal.

Sissy saw Mr. Harrelson and Mr. Workman exchange looks as they greeted each other, looks that said the dog probably wasn't going to make it.

Mr. Workman stood at his son's shoulder. "Do you recognize this animal, son?"

"No, sir." Elijah squinted. "I don't think. Maybe… Vince Cory's dogs look kind of like this."

Again, that grim look between the adults.

"What?" Sissy said. "What is it? She can go to

the veterinarian. My family will pay. I know they will."

"But, honey, who's going to take her afterward?" Mr. Harrelson asked reasonably.

"I will," Sissy said. She suspected her parents might not be keen on this, but it was clear Mr. Harrelson wanted to put her out of her misery.

Elijah said, "How did she get like that?"

The adults exchanged another look. Elijah gazed up at his father, and Sissy saw some kind of dawning recognition come over his own face. "Not… You think she got in a fight?"

"That's one way to put it," his father said.

Mr. Harrelson turned and walked toward a car that had driven up to the pumps, but Sissy had the feeling that was just an excuse to leave, to get away from the topic, to not talk about it.

"Dogfights," she said, suddenly understanding. "Pit fights. That's what happened, isn't it, Mr. Workman?"

Elijah looked stricken. As though many revelations were coming to him suddenly, all at once.

His father said, "Let's see if we can get this old girl into the back of the truck. We'll see what Dr. Fisher has to say about her."

CHAPTER TWO

My first dog, Lucky, had been the victim of
a staged dogfight. I called her Lucky because
a veterinarian was able to save her, despite
her injuries.

—*On the Side of the Dogs,* Elijah Workman,
2008

Echo Springs, Missouri
April 10, 1959

"YOU'RE SPENDING an awful lot of time with
Elijah Workman," Sissy's mother said.

"So? We're friends." Granted, no more than
friends, which Sissy found discouraging. She and
her mother were cleaning the kennels, then her
mother planned to take the dogs entered in the following weekend's show around the practice ring.
It wasn't really big enough for German shepherds
to stretch out, but it was better than nothing.

Heloise Atherton studied her daughter briefly,

then began to spread fresh straw in Ruby's kennel run. "Just as long as that's all it is."

Sissy's pulse quickened. Did her mother think that Elijah might regard her as a girlfriend? Sissy dearly wished he would and rather liked the thought that others might consider the two of them that way. But what was her mother's problem with Elijah? "What if it was different?" she asked as though simply curious.

Heloise paused. Her daughters had inherited their height from her. She was a powerful presence, especially in the obedience or conformation ring. The Athertons expected and delivered excellence, whatever it took. Blond like her daughters, she wore her hair one length, drawn back with a headband or swept up in a neat French twist. Sissy could tell that her mother was carefully choosing her words now.

"Oh, I just think you'd be happier dating a different type of boy, someone whose family is more like yours."

Sissy processed this. "What's wrong with Elijah?" she finally said, determined to defend him. "He's the best-looking boy in my class and a good student, and he's been earning money since he was eight years old."

"I know, I know." Her mother shook her head at Sissy. "There's no need to overreact. But in a few years you'll be going away to college and you'll meet all sorts of people from backgrounds similar to your own."

"This is because he's poor?" Sissy said in disbelief.

"No, not that. Darling, it doesn't seem important to you now, but little things may matter to you later. For instance, if a person says, 'I says' or 'So I tells him.'"

Sissy tried to remember if Elijah ever spoke that way. She knew his father did. Her mother was right about one thing; it didn't seem important.

"Think what his uncle is like," Heloise said. "Imagine him being *your* relative. Do they even have a telephone?"

Sissy scoffed. She could remember when the Workmans hadn't had a phone, either. "Of course they do." No television, though, and his father's work truck the only car. "Elijah's smart," she insisted. "Anyway, to set your mind at rest, I don't think he knows I'm a girl."

Her mother said nothing. Rather than seeming satisfied by this, she just appeared more quietly fretful, as though something very troubling was brewing beneath her calm exterior.

A few minutes later, as she let Ruby into the run, she said, "Sissy, my ugly duckling, I don't think you realize yet that you are becoming the loveliest of swans."

Eldon, Missouri
June 13, 1959

"How do I look?" Sissy demanded, pirouetting for Elijah, an action he found completely at odds with her appearance. Tight pink pants, black leather jacket, lots of bright red lipstick and black mascara, her hair, naturally straight, in a high ponytail. "Cheap?" she inquired.

Actually, Elijah thought she looked sexy but still a little too upmarket for where they were headed. And he was furious that she was here. "How did you get out of the house like that?"

"Changed at a gas station outside Echo Springs."

"You know you could blow this entire thing. You're not supposed to be here."

"Nobody in Eldon knows me, and I want to be part of this. I'm the whole reason *you're* here."

"I don't want to be here," he said. "I'm only here because I have to be." He held Satchmo's leash. The dog was lean, muscular and strangely eager. He knew what they were there to do, and the dog was keen for it.

Which didn't make it remotely all right.

Sissy was certainly right that she was why Elijah was at the pit fight at Jackson's Dock. It was Sissy who'd found Lucky, after all. Lucky, who had been so disfigured in a staged dogfight. Lucky had become Elijah's first dog. And Elijah and Sissy had become friends. Sort of.

This had been her idea. *You can do something about it, Elijah. You can find out from your uncle where the fights are.*

At first he hadn't believed he could do it. Deceive Uncle Silas? Not to mention his own parents? The first thing he would have to hide was that he was interested in dogfights. Then he would have to tell Uncle Silas that he *was* interested in dogfights—and yet not explain why.

He'd told Sissy he didn't think these were nice people.

It had taken him a year to work up his courage, then another year of being taken into his uncle's confidence without once being invited to a pit fight. During that time, he'd learned a lot about himself—that he could become someone else at will. He felt anger toward his uncle; Silas Workman wasn't the person Elijah had believed him to be. Ella had died as the result of a staged fight. When he was alone, Elijah had wept about this, and then he'd very coolly assume a false enthusiasm for fights, determined to find a way to stop them.

Finally, not knowing what to do if he could find out where dogs were being matched, he had gone to the Humane Society in Osage Beach with Sissy. Her father had driven them, convinced that they simply wanted to volunteer there. Elijah had persuaded him not to talk about it with Elijah's parents, saying it might cause some conflict in his own family. He just, he said, wanted to see what it was all about.

Deceiving Mr. Atherton was definitely the worst.

After three visits to the place, Sissy and Elijah met a man named Don Slocum, who was an agent for the Humane Society. His job was investigating animal abuse. He'd agreed that the dogfights were illegal, but said the Humane Society didn't have the resources to address the issue.

But if they were illegal, Sissy insisted, couldn't they make sure the people were arrested?

Don had at last decided that the people staging the fights might be required to pay some fines. He said again and again that it was "a big problem," but that children could not make a difference.

Elijah had suggested he could gather information that Don might find useful. Then he had begun riding along with Don when the agent investigated animal shelters.

Now, Don knew about the match in Eldon.

Elijah had to go to the match because his uncle had persuaded him to take Satchmo there. Uncle Silas planned to match one of his other dogs in Arkansas. There would be no bust at that match, but a friend of Don's would be present, trying to learn more about the dogfighting network. They needed to tap Silas Workman for all they could get, and Elijah was their link. Don was going to arrest Elijah at the match and call his parents.

Elijah hadn't quite worked out what he was going to tell them.

Don Slocum worried that Elijah's father might reveal the truth to his brother. Still, he'd said, "I can't tell you what to do, Elijah. If you want me to talk with your parents and explain everything, I'll certainly do it."

"Which one is this?" Sissy looked at Satchmo with slight distaste, Elijah thought.

"It's Satchmo, and if you can't pretend he's the handsomest dog you've ever seen, you better get out of here."

"I can pull it off. Here's my story—I'm your girlfriend, and this is all a big secret. I want to come to the dogfight because it's exciting, different from my other life. I want to be a bad girl, and I'm crazy about my boyfriend because he's a bad boy. He has the baddest dog in Missouri. Right?"

Well, she'd certainly created a role for herself.

"Whatever," he said. He was nervous about going in, nervous about any possible harm that might come to Satchmo in a fight, afraid of what he would see. And he couldn't risk blowing everything by arguing with Sissy Atherton in this hot, dusty parking lot.

To his amazement, Sissy opened the black patent leather purse she carried and withdrew a pack of cigarettes.

Elijah rolled his eyes and headed for the lakeside shack that was known as Jackson's Dock.

SISSY SUPPOSED she'd expected snarling dogs. When the German shepherd bitches of Echo Springs Farm fought, they generally did some snarling.

But these dogs weren't big on that apparently.

Everything she'd believed about the kinds of people who staged dogfights was borne out by the crowd at Jackson's Dock. She saw one other girl her age; she was missing a front tooth. The people looked impoverished, mean or both. Some of the men appeared frankly dangerous.

Elijah didn't stick out, though she'd been sure he would. He always struck her as clean-cut, certainly the type of boy her father would be happy for her to date, if her mother felt differently. He did look nervous, but it seemed perfectly normal—a tall, hawk-nosed teenage boy in a place he wasn't supposed to be, doing something he'd been forbidden to do.

Sissy knew she would have to work at self-control. She would want to rescue any dog that was being hurt, and she knew she must not attempt to do that. A sheriff would come, and *he* would save the dogs and arrest the people staging the dogfight. She supposed she could expect to be arrested as well. That seemed exciting to her, and it was certainly for a good cause.

Sissy was here because she cared about dogs.

She was also here because if Elijah spent enough time around her, perhaps he'd begin to think of her differently and it might occur to him to ask her to the Kickoff Dance in September.

Elijah, unfortunately, didn't seem terribly interested in her, and why should he be? She was skinny and didn't tan, and her eyelashes and eyebrows were so light, they just blended in with her skin. She had a long face and she was too tall. She'd seen Elijah looking at her friend Lucia D'Angelo, who was voluptuous and looked like a movie star.

Sissy was going to have to get by on her personality.

Right now Elijah didn't appear to be thinking of girls at all, only about his uncle's dog, whom Elijah was holding by his wide collar, though he had a leash on him as well.

Satchmo appeared to be all muscle, a little too lean, in Sissy's opinion. Elijah agreed. He'd told her that when his uncle's dogs were "in the keep," in other words training for a fight, they spent hours endurance-building on homemade treadmills.

Elijah remained against a back wall with Satchmo, who was not one of the first dogs to be matched. Deciding to make her own way in this unfamiliar world, Sissy headed down to the pit. It smelled of beer and cigarette smoke and the occasional person in serious need of a bath. She saw a timer and another person she supposed was a referee. Neither of these individuals would have been allowed within an AKC ring as they were dressed, one in a white tank-style undershirt like her father wore under his business shirts, the other wearing a shirt with an embroidered pocket identifying him as "Mean Moe." The timer was smoking a cigarette, holding it between his thumb and forefinger like a tough.

A man beside Sissy looked her up and down, grinned, then looked away.

She lit a cigarette. She *did* know how to smoke, as this was something she and her friends did when her parents weren't around.

There was a coin toss, and a red-haired man with peeling lips and many freckles and scabs began washing a white pit bull-type dog.

Sissy peered around the group. There were only a few women, most of them hard-looking, but some simply could have been wives and mothers.

It shocked her that women would enjoy seeing dogs tear each other to pieces. Already her own stomach had begun to flutter in apprehension of what was about to happen.

The other dog was also white but with brindle spots. This one was skinnier than Satchmo—muscular but too skinny.

Finally the fight began, and Sissy was stunned by the fury with which the dogs leaped at each other, stunned by the tenacity with which one latched on to the other's ear.

She started to feel sick. How would it look if she turned away from the spectacle? She glanced around to see what Elijah was doing.

He still leaned against the wall, now talking to a middle-aged man who needed a shave. They were both watching the pit. How long would this go on for before the Humane Society people or the police, whoever was coming to save the dogs, arrived?

Blood.

Seeing Lucky the day Sissy had found her, Sissy knew she should have been prepared for the blood. The owner of Jackson's Dock wandered to the edge of the pit but also glanced regularly toward the door. A man in a black leather jacket beside Sissy gave her a nasty smile. He held a black pit bull on a lead. He was handsome but frightening. He wore his hair in a DA style, and he had long sideburns.

Sissy knew she should try to act her part. She tried to pet his dog, but it snapped at her.

"He's mean," the man told her.

Sissy glanced back at the ring and wished she hadn't. The white dog with the brindle spots was bleeding profusely from its face, and she thought she might faint.

It seemed to go on too long, until a whistle blew. The man with the black leather jacket told her that one of the dogs had "turned," but Sissy didn't understand. He was telling her that it was the all-white dog's turn to "scratch," whatever that meant.

Legs shaking, she eased back from the pit to join Elijah, who was now crouched beside Satchmo, looking apprehensive.

The double doors suddenly flew open, and a slight stirring went through the crowd.

"Everyone stay where you are." Two sheriff's deputies walked in, as people poured out of the dockside doors, ignoring the officers' command.

Sissy knew Elijah was supposed to be arrested now. Instead, he grabbed her hand. Ducking beside Satchmo, he dragged her into the crowd and away from the deputies.

"WEREN'T YOU supposed to get arrested?"

"Don said I *might*." They sat on rocks at the water's edge a quarter mile from Jackson's Dock.

The problem with not being arrested was that he'd lost his ride home. Normally he would have hitch-hiked, but he was worried about doing so with Satchmo. People in the area would know he'd been at the fight, might turn him in, and he'd rather avoid that. One of his uncle's friends had driven him and Satchmo to Jackson's Dock, but Elijah had no idea where the man was now.

"How did you get there?" he asked Sissy.

"Allie Morgan."

"You told her?" exclaimed Elijah.

"Of course not. I had her drop me at Eldon Ice Cream. I told her I was meeting someone."

"Did you tell her who?"

"Well, yes." Even in the dark, he could see her whole face darken, flooding with color. "It's not like we're dating, and she knows that."

Elijah didn't want to talk about this. Sissy was attractive—well, more than she used to be—but his big problem was that he was supposed to be out feeding dogs, his bike was at his uncle's house and he and Sissy Atherton were stranded. He'd be lucky if her father didn't kill him. Who did he know with a car?

Sissy said, "I could call Kennedy."

Elijah shot a look at her. "Is she around? Wouldn't she tell your parents?"

"I don't think so."

"Don't you think you'll be in less trouble if you're alone? I mean, I'll wait with you until Kennedy gets here," he said, knowing this was what he should do. He couldn't leave her alone. "But won't it be worse if you're with me?"

"I don't care," Sissy said. "And I've caught her sneaking in late. We'll be even."

Uneasily Elijah agreed.

"I CANNOT BELIEVE you were with Elijah Workman." Kennedy's diatribe started the minute she pulled the Thunderbird away from the Workmans' crowded two-story house, crowded cheek-to-jowl with others just like it, in West Echo Springs. Because Elijah was running late, when they'd reached his uncle's house and he'd left Satchmo there, Kennedy had agreed to put his bicycle in the trunk and drive him home. He could say a friend had given him a lift.

"There is nothing wrong with Elijah!" Sissy exclaimed. She'd not had to argue this point since that one conversation with her mother weeks before, but she really couldn't see the big deal. "Dad likes him."

"Dad likes him as a dog-sitter. Not as a boyfriend for one of his daughters."

"I wish he was my boyfriend," Sissy muttered. Kennedy glanced at her with a look of appraisal and pity. "You wish that *now,* but trust me, the older you get, the more you'll be grateful your wish never came true."

Sissy considered that, hoping her sister was right. Yet somehow she doubted she would ever feel that way about Elijah, that she would ever get over him, that she would ever *not* want what she wanted right now.

Echo Springs, Missouri
May 2, 1961

IT WAS ALMOST the end of junior year, and Elijah had been drinking beer, which was unusual for him, and Lucia D'Angelo was sitting beside him in her yellow-and-black polka-dot bikini. The party was at Allie Morgan's family's lakeside cabin, which was three cabins down from the Athertons'. Two families who could afford to own *two* homes in Echo Springs. The Morgans were out of town, and the Athertons were at their farm, so the party was a secret from the adults.

Elijah watched the fireflies, thinking that he'd like to kiss Lucia, like to put his hand in her bikini top, like to do more than that. His whole life his parents, his aunts and uncles, the priests at church—everyone—had emphasized that sex would happen *after* marriage and that everything leading up to sex would also happen then. Elijah figured a little fooling around wasn't as sinister as people said. He had kissed other girls, had messed around a bit on double dates when someone had a car (he never did). He also believed that Lucia had done a lot more than fool around in the back seat of Tom Riordan's Thunderbird before Tom went off to play football for the University of Iowa. Nonetheless, something held Elijah back from pursuing her, even from kissing her.

He gazed down the Morgans' dock and watched Sissy Atherton dive gracefully into the lake. Her swimsuit was a one-piece, all white. You could tell her class, that was for sure. More and more, she reminded him of a movie star—Grace Kelly, for instance—not exactly in looks but in style. He knew that when it came to marriage, he wanted someone like Sissy, who dated but whom he was sure remained a virgin, and a virgin with strict limits.

He stood up from the low stone wall where he'd been sitting. "I'm going in the water."

It was 7:00 p.m. and still light out. Jay Morgan and Evan Chamberlain were down on the dock, talking to Sissy's friend Anne Beth.

"Me, too," Lucia said, bouncing to her feet, her ample breasts nearly spilling from her bikini top.

But Elijah realized he wanted to talk to Sissy, with whom he talked little these days. They'd grown apart in the past year. She was spending time with her ballet, he thought, and doing whatever people did at the country club. Someone had said she was going to teach swimming there this summer, not because she had to work, but probably because the country club would only hire someone like her, someone who was one of them.

It seemed a lifetime ago that they used to talk about dogs and that they'd been at Jackson's Dock together. That had been Elijah's last dogfight experience. He'd continued to volunteer for the Humane Society, taking care of dogs at the local shelter. There was nothing to stop him asking Sissy out. Sure, he lived in a less affluent part of town, but he came from a good family. His parents had high expectations for him and his brothers and sisters. They'd all been taught to work hard, in and out of school, and he certainly planned to succeed in life.

In any case, he was a good student and a basketball player, and he'd always been accepted by the other guys in his class.

"You going to the prom?" Lucia asked as they headed down the dock.

Elijah did not look at her. He knew she was

hinting that they should go together, but he didn't plan to ask her in any case. *Except to kiss her and put your hands down her top, Elijah?* The thought was tempting. But then she would be his girlfriend, he supposed, and he didn't really want her for his girlfriend.

"Not planning on it. I think I'll be busy." He was sure he'd be busy because he always was—if not earning money or studying, then playing basketball with his brothers or helping his father.

Lucia understood everything he hadn't said. With a wave that carefully hid any resentment of his disinterest, she strolled ahead of him to the end of the dock. Anne Beth had joined Sissy in the water, and the two girls were swimming out to the wooden raft moored fifty feet from the end of the dock.

Jay wolf-whistled at Lucia and said, "Decided to share your charms with us, Lucia?" He and Evan had been mixing martinis earlier, but had now dispensed with cocktail glasses, if not their chosen beverage, in favor of large plastic cups.

Elijah slowed slightly, putting more distance between himself and Lucia D'Angelo.

Lucia said, "What charms you is nothing I intend to share."

Evan scoffed, exchanging a look with Jay.

"And what's that supposed to mean?" she asked.

"We know you *like* to share," said Evan.

Elijah reached the end of the dock just behind Lucia, planning to dive in and get away from this conversation. Evan and Jay were drunk, and Evan reeked of gin.

Lucia glared at the other boys. "Whatever you fantasize about has nothing to do with reality."

"Reality has everything to do with quantity," said Evan, "and nothing to do with quality."

Elijah paused at the edge of the dock, uneasy. Evan was a jerk, but he was going pretty far. *Sticks and stones, Elijah. She can take care of herself.*

"Quantity," Jay said, "or money. Money isn't the same as quality, which some people never seem to get. Anyone can make money."

For some reason, Elijah wondered if this was directed at him. He and Jay had never had a problem in the past.

"And some people really know how to sell themselves," Evan answered his friend in a tone which might have been joking, if not for the ugly implication.

Elijah turned around. "Why don't you cool it, Evan?"

"Oh. You're taking your turn?" Evan said, truly sounding as though offending Elijah had been the last thing he'd wanted to do. "Sorry, man. Didn't realize. Hell, sorry all around."

Elijah didn't like the implication that he was "taking his turn" with Lucia, and didn't want to leave things that way. "Doesn't have anything to do with me," he said. "But you owe Lucia an apology."

Jay stood up slowly and leaned against one of the pilings near the Morgans' berthed speedboat. He muttered, "Not worth your trouble, Elijah."

This seemed both a warning and a mollifying suggestion.

Evan shrugged. "It's not like I said anything that's news."

Elijah felt Lucia edging back from the boys, putting him between her and them. "Let it go, Elijah. They're not worth it."

"Because we won't give you your price?" Evan said.

This wasn't his fight. It was Tom Riordan's fault, for behaving in a way that could get Lucia talked about.

But Lucia lived one block from Elijah. He'd known her since she was five years old, and she went to his church. They'd been through First Communion and confirmation together. Suddenly it felt as though Evan were treating one of Elijah's own sisters this way.

He took a step toward Evan. "Apologize to Lucia, *now*."

"Let it go, Elijah," Lucia whispered urgently, not like a girl who enjoyed boys fighting over her.

Evan stood up, swaying slightly. "I don't think I will, Workman. She can leave if she feels out of her depth. Socially, you know."

Jay said, "Guys, let's just cool it. Elijah, he didn't mean it."

Elijah repeated, "Apologize." He knew he was leaving Evan no options. He could back down and apologize, or—

Evan tried to shove Elijah, but Elijah was faster and just stepped to the side. Evan swung at him. From above, somebody yelled, "Fight!"

EVAN'S VOICE HAD CARRIED easily across the water. Clinging to the edge of the raft, Sissy and Anne Beth watched the scene on the dock apprehensively. Anne Beth hissed, "Evan's such a creep."

Sissy said, "Elijah's doing the white-knight thing."

Both had seen Evan throw the first punch, which didn't connect. The second had the same result. Elijah evaded him, saying something else they couldn't hear.

"Fight! Fight! Fight!" came a chant from above.

"This is awful," Sissy says. "I don't want to go back there."

"Let's swim to the beach instead," Anne Beth suggested. "Those guys are drunk. I don't want to be here anymore."

"Let's see what happens." Sissy felt anxious on behalf of Elijah, slightly less so for Lucia. Evan Chamberlain could become ugly. She'd seen it before at the country club.

"Sissy, we should go," Anne Beth repeated.

Jay grabbed Evan's shoulders. "Easy, Ev. Let's forget this, everyone. Elijah, take a walk."

This time, Sissy heard Elijah. Never taking his eyes from Evan, he said, "Get your things, Lucia." He nodded to Jay, took Lucia's hand and started up the dock.

"Are they dating?" Anne Beth asked. "Why did he back down?"

"He didn't." Sissy lived with a pack of dogs. She'd seen the unspoken warning in the direction of Elijah's gaze and in his stance. "He just knows Evan's drunk and a moron and not worth it." Just the way her parents' champion Tide never bothered to fight Warren; a cold stare was enough. "Come on, let's go. We can give them a ride."

Anne Beth said, "I doubt they want company."

Sissy exclaimed, "Oh, puh-leeze. He'd never go for her."

Sissy HAD NOT WANTED a Thunderbird for her six-teenth birthday. She had wanted a Corvette.

But she had received a turquoise Thunderbird and was delighted all the same. She'd driven Anne Beth to the party, and now she was taking Elijah and Lucia home. She'd dropped them off in order. Anne Beth's house had been closest, then Lucia's.

And now she and Elijah sat in the idling car outside Lucia's house.

"Do you need to get right home?" Sissy asked.

Elijah glanced up, startled. "No. What about you?"

"I feel like having an adventure," she said. "We could go to the Strip. We could go see the fish at the dam."

"Kind of iffy down there this time of night," Elijah replied.

"No, it's not. We can get fudge."

"Okay," he agreed, and she saw his straight white teeth as he grinned in the dark.

The Workmans even go to the orthodontist, she thought, still mentally arguing with her mother's opinion of the family. Not that they'd discussed it lately. Sissy hadn't seen Elijah for months, except at school and sometimes at parties.

"Want to drive?" she asked.

"You trust me?"

"Definitely. After all, you didn't swing at Evan. That was good judgment."

His smile seemed slightly chagrined. "Why's that?"

"Because he'd never forget it, and he'd act like a jerk to you for the rest of forever. That was nice of you, by the way." Instead of getting out of the car, she stood up in her seat in her white pedal pushers and pale blue blouse. "Let's switch seats."

Elijah crawled under her, and she stepped over him, giving him a chance to admire her ankles.

"You've always liked Lucia, haven't you?" she asked airily, settling in the passenger seat and finding the seat belt. "Seat belts," she said. "It's a family rule."

Elijah obediently found his and adjusted it to fit him. He switched on the turn indicator, looked out in the street and pulled away from the curb. "She's just a friend," he said.

Sissy tossed her shoulder-length, straight hair, still wet from swimming.

"In any case," she said, "Evan's a clown, and he's obnoxious, and I'm glad you didn't get in a fight." *And I was right,* she thought, *that Elijah and Lucia aren't that way about each other. Well, maybe she is about* him.

Sissy, on the other hand, was over Elijah Workman. Well, over the way she used to be about him. Right now, he was interesting primarily because he was the kind of person her mother wanted her to have nothing to do with.

"Go over the dam," she instructed.

"Why?"

"Because my parents are at the club, and they'll come back over HH."

He'd reached a Stop sign, and when he'd come to a halt he looked over at her. "You mean, you're not supposed to be doing this?"

"No," she insisted. "I just mean that I'll have to listen to…" she sought for the right words and settled on "…advice."

He did not pull ahead. The street was quiet, no one behind them.

"About what?"

Why must he be so annoyingly direct? And what could she say? She wasn't about to tell him that her mother wouldn't want her spending time with him. Her dad might not even be crazy about the idea. Of course, her dad wasn't crazy about her having a boyfriend at all. Instead, he encouraged her to learn all about the colleges she might want to go to. He had the right idea; she knew what she wanted, and she wasn't going to let a boyfriend stand in her way.

"My father's worried I'm going to get a boyfriend," she decided to say.

"Ah." Elijah thought this over for a moment, then edged the Thunderbird forward. "If that's all."

THEY SAT on one of the docks near the fudge shop, each with a Coke, and let their feet dangle in the lake. Sissy had fed coins into the jukebox inside, and they could hear it playing "Blue Moon" by the Marcels.

"Do you still show your dog?" Elijah asked her. "In Obedience?" Over the years, he'd learned some of the terminology of the American Kennel Club.

"No. I tried to get his UD—Utility Dog—for a while but we weren't having much luck. And I've been busy."

"You were in the play," he said.

"Yes. That's what I'm going to do. I want to study performing arts, acting and dance. That's what I love best. What about you?"

Elijah shrugged. His father drummed it into his head every day that it was good to be *practical*, and what interested Elijah was animals. His father had said, "Then, become a veterinarian," but that wasn't precisely what Elijah was hoping to do. He wanted to know why animals behaved the way they did. "I'm not sure. Something with animals." He confessed, "I could be happy watching them all day, trying to figure out what's going on in their heads." He quoted something he held in his head always. "'They are not brethren, they are not underlings; they are other nations, caught with ourselves in the net of life and time, fellow prisoners of the splendor and travail of the earth.' Henry Beston."

Sissy turned, stared at his profile as he looked out on the dark lake. Finally, he looked back, and she said, "Say that again."

He smiled, that dazzling, wolfish smile and repeated the quotation.

"Will you please write that down for me?" she asked.

"Sure." He looked at her for a moment. "I suppose you have your date for the prom lined up."

She nodded and suddenly laughed, confident and far from the ugly duckling of their junior high school days. "But just for future reference—I would have said yes."

Elijah grinned, a bit mischievously. "What if I asked to kiss you?"

A smile curved her wide, beautiful lips, showing her dimples, which, when combined with her well-defined cheekbones, gave her a unique loveliness. Braces gone, straight white teeth. "That would be quite interesting."

Elijah searched her violet eyes. "I'm asking."

She grinned at him. "Yes, Elijah Workman."

He had to touch her hair, push it back from her

creamy skin. Touch one pale eyebrow. "You're really beautiful, Sissy. You're…classy."

She winced.

"What?" he asked.

She looked pained. "When someone says someone is 'classy'…"

Elijah suddenly understood. "It's a sign that he's not?"

She gave him a smile that asked forgiveness for the observation.

"I'll remember," he said, and he kissed her mouth, felt her lips move under his, kissing him back. The girl had kissed before. And by the time they drew apart for a moment, he knew something else.

Sissy Atherton liked him.

A lot.

The music on the jukebox changed to the Everly Brothers' "Let It Be Me."

She said, "Will you dance with me, Elijah?"

"Here?" He looked around the deserted dock, stood up and reached for her hand.

Then, she was dancing in his arms on the dock in the moonlight and saying, "Don't you think this is the most beautiful song? I'm a very romantic person, Elijah."

She said this with the impish smile that took his breath.

Suddenly blessing the day he'd found her and afraid of the strength of that feeling, he said, "Yeah. Me, too."

Echo Springs, Missouri
February 8, 1962

IT WASN'T Sissy's parents' way to forbid her to date a particular boy, especially when the boy wasn't a high school dropout showing up on a motorcycle, smoking cigarettes, with a fifth of vodka in the pocket of his leather jacket. Instead, her mother, in particular, became increasingly and subtly cool toward Elijah Workman and created situations in which she believed Elijah would be out of his element and would show his gaucheness.

Encouraging Elijah and Sissy to have their pre-Valentine dance dinner at the Echo Springs Country Club was one of these ideas. Elijah had begun to notice the trend—and wondered about it. Much of the comfort he'd felt with Mr. Atherton when he was young and dog-sitting for the Athertons had disappeared. In fact, the Athertons had found "a nice girl we know" to take care of the dogs when the family went to shows.

Sissy said, "You would go as our family's guest. I mean, you and I would have our own table, and my parents, theirs."

He and Sissy walked along the shore in front of the Athertons' lakeside cabin, bundled against the cold. The Athertons were spending the weekend in the cabin, and Sissy had invited Elijah to come down for the afternoon and for dinner. He had refused the dinner invitation, saying he needed to study.

Now he knew he had to do more. "Sissy, this isn't really working."

"What?" she asked, glancing over at him. She wore a white angora beret over her bright yellow hair. She was so tall, model-thin and elegant. He was tall, too, six feet, but he didn't feel elegant. He had the family's beaky nose and he always shaved immediately before seeing Sissy, but the hair on his face seemed to grow so fast and dark.

"Sissy, your folks don't like me."

"Yes, they—"

He shook his head, stopping her. "And I don't like the way things are going. I don't own a car. We're always going places in yours. If I were to take someone else out, I'd borrow my dad's truck, if he'd lend it. If we were going to a dance, I'd pick a restaurant where I was welcome."

"You're welcome at the—"

"But I don't belong. Don't you see? And Sissy, you're going away in the fall, and with my dad being sick. I have obligations here."

His father had some kind of lung ailment and had been in and out of the hospital.

"You're saying you want to break up with me," Sissy said, sounding a little shocked.

"I'm saying that it doesn't really matter what anyone wants. We're on different paths."

Sissy glanced at him. She'd always suspected that Elijah didn't like her as much as she liked him. Sexually they were on the same page. He was as eager as anyone, though also conscious about, maybe troubled by, how far things were going, seeming more protective of her virginity than she felt. When he'd once choked out that they needed to stop, Sissy had wanted to ask why, but had a feeling Elijah might think less of her, so she'd agreed.

Yes, Elijah was very straitlaced and Sissy *was* excited about going to Sarah Lawrence in the fall. She knew her life would change then. But Elijah was so darn… handsome? More than that. There was something about him that would not let her go.

Now, however, she would have to let go.

He stopped walking on the rocky beach dotted with patches of snow and looked at her. "Sissy, things are getting too serious between us. If our futures were going in the same direction, I'd want to marry you. But you have other plans, and you should follow them."

"You have plans, too!" she cried. Elijah had been admitted to several colleges, had won two scholarships. He wanted to study animal behavior, maybe teach someday.

He shook his head. "Sissy, my father is *dying*. I hope he won't, and my mother doesn't know just how sick he is, and I'd like you to keep the information to yourself. It's something Dad has told me because he wants to make sure my mother and my brothers and sisters are cared for."

"You're going to sacrifice everything for them?" She heard her own words, heard how self-serving they sounded—perhaps she was being childish wishing that Elijah would serve his own desires first.

"It's not a sacrifice," he said sharply.

Sissy could hardly believe he felt that way. If he did—well, they really were pretty different. Still… She drew herself up. "Well, I get the point. Do you want me to drive you home?"

He shook his head. "I'll hitch." The way he'd gotten there. Hitchhiking and walking from the road.

Her mouth formed a grim little line. "I guess I'll see you at school then."

He nodded, looked as though he wanted to say something. Or ask something. But eventually he turned away.

Elijah knew that if he told Sissy what he wanted, she would grant it. And she would never understand why he didn't ask, why it wasn't right. There was no future for them. So why should he ask for one last kiss?

A Coca-Cola truck stopped for him, and when Elijah opened the door, he heard the Everly Brothers on the radio, singing the first song he and Sissy had ever danced to.

CHAPTER THREE

A hearing-impaired woman brought her service dog to Mass. While the congregation sang, I happened to glance at the animal and found him gazing at her with a rapt and joyful expression. I remembered the howls of our German shepherds, their spontaneous singing.

Perhaps they howl to praise.

—*Among the God Dogs,* Elijah Workman, 1990

Kansas City, Missouri
June 1, 1969

AN AMERICAN KENNEL CLUB DOG SHOW was an unusual place to find an undercover operative for the Midwest Region of the Humane Society, but that was where twenty-five-year-old Elijah Workman ended up, searching out a dog thief. The thefts would not have come to the attention of the Humane Society were it not for one of the stolen dogs being found dead.

The case was ugly, and the Humane Society was liaising with the Federal Bureau of Investigation. Before his mother began working in an insurance office in Echo Springs, Elijah had served as a sheriff's deputy. Then the Humane Society had recruited him, and he'd become one of their highest-paid investigators, which admittedly still earned him less than he'd made as a cop.

Special Agent Paul Hilliard, who'd left the Echo Springs Sheriff's Department to join the FBI, was tracking the thief because the torture and death of the dog seemed connected to some murders occurring in the same area and at the same time. Other FBI agents were nearby, as well, in case they found the perpetrator on the premises.

Another member of the team was Barbara Watson, a Humane Society representative from the regional office, who was on hand to take care of any stolen dogs to which their quarry led them. If they found the person they sought. Barbara was also undercover, but she was miserable in that role—or so Elijah felt.

Paul and Elijah were dressed as handlers in pastel jackets, white shirts, ties and good trousers, and Paul was escorting his Boxer, Odysseus, who was an AKC champion entered in the show, all which improved their cover. On the way to the show, Elijah had asked Paul if the FBI had ever noticed that the kinds of people who hurt animals often also liked to hurt people. In his line of work, Elijah *had* noticed this. People, however, could sometimes take care of themselves.

Animals could not.

Paul said he *personally* had noted the point, but he didn't think the Bureau as a whole subscribed to the idea.

Barbara, a blonde with a very round face and wrists almost as big as Elijah's, was dressed as a groomer, wearing trousers and a blouse with a blue smock over them.

"Now look at that," Paul said to Elijah in an undertone. "Ring two."

Distracted momentarily from watching the grooming area, where several of the thefts had occurred at previous shows, Elijah glanced toward the ring where a tall blonde in a pale blue suit and high heels, her hair in a French twist, ran around a ring with an Afghan Hound, other Afghan Hounds surrounding them. The shade of hair, like sweet corn, drew Elijah's attention, making him think immediately of Sissy.

She had great legs and a tall, statuesque figure. *It's got to be Sissy.* He wished he had eyes in the back of his head, so he could wait till she turned around. Instead, he had to watch the grooming area. The thief and probable murderer seemed to hit the biggest shows in the area. All, so far, had been Midwestern shows.

How in hell did he do it? Most groomers were women; the few men stood out. Elijah found it hard to believe that no one would notice an unfamiliar man taking a dog from the show. A man dressed as a handler maybe? Or an actual handler?

In the car on the way to the show, Barbara had said, "Those AKC people are capable of anything."

Barbara believed that the American Kennel Club was the root of all evil, insisting that people shouldn't breed dogs when there were so many unwanted animals languishing in pounds around the country. Her anti-AKC prejudice was one reason Elijah would have preferred to take along a different officer, but that decision had been in someone else's hands.

Elijah watched a middle-aged red-haired woman wearing a pink smock over her clothing brush a handsome Samoyed. She worked near the edge of the area, not far from the handwritten sign which read: WARNING: LEAVE NO DOG UNATTENDED! BEWARE OF DOG THIEVES!

If people followed those instructions, the dog thief would be stuck, which was why Barbara was here working on an Alaskan malamute named Whiteout who had wound up at the pound and was posing as a show dog. Elijah thought he looked good, but Paul had said his conformation was lousy. Nonetheless, Whiteout was their bait. "I doubt he'll tempt our man," Paul had said, though he'd flatly refused to allow them to use Odysseus as the lure.

Elijah studied the redheaded groomer. She kept craning her neck to try to see the far ring, and he suspected she might step away from the Samoyed for a dangerous moment.

Before that happened, however, Barbara, in a very convincing manner, tossed down a comb in irritation, hunted through her capacious tote bag for another, then stalked away from Whiteout, heading for a vending booth that sold grooming tools.

Paul was still watching the blonde in ring two, and Elijah pretended to participate. "Barbara's left."

Though the last time he'd seen her had been three years before at a breakfast after church, Elijah had no trouble recognizing Sissy. His heart lurched. *Is her family now breeding Afghans?* he wondered. Or maybe Sissy was working as a paid handler.

He made himself look away, turning at an angle to Paul so that he could see both the Samoyed's table and Whiteout's.

The woman with the Samoyed did leave. She strode through the grooming area, stopped at Whiteout's table and removed the restraints keeping him there. Whiteout licked her face as she hauled him off the table, snapped on a lead and started toward the exit farthest from Paul and Elijah. Paul slipped away from Elijah's side to follow her.

Whiteout, however, had his own ideas. He stopped in his tracks, briefly sniffed the groomer's legs, and lifted one of his own to pee on her.

Whiteout's cover was blown. This was not show dog behavior.

A groomer at the next table told the thief, "He does that in the ring, he gets no score."

"Not my dog," said the redhead with a convincing rolling of eyes.

No one else seemed to notice anything amiss. Elijah headed in the opposite direction around the grooming area, past where a family sat eating hot dogs and watching Yorkshire Terriers in the ring.

Elijah couldn't see the thief and decided she must have gone the other way. What he did see was a big-pawed white blur dragging a blue lead snatch a partially consumed hot dog from a toddler, who instantly wailed in terror and distress. After one gulp, Whiteout began to lick the sobbing child's face. The mother set down her own food to rescue her child, and Whiteout ate that, too.

"Loose dog! Loose dog!" someone on the other side of the Yorkie ring yelled. Elijah had no doubt that the thief would abandon Whiteout now that he'd drawn so much attention to himself, and Elijah was right. She'd disappeared, probably returning to her Samoyed.

Someone needed to grab Whiteout, but Elijah didn't want to be seen with the canine outlaw and blow his own cover.

The father of the hot dog family set down his food to grab the renegade, who seized that unexpected offering, too, before making his getaway—into the Yorkshire Terrier ring.

A judge screamed, "Someone grab that dog!" while eight Yorkshire Terrier handlers snatched up their charges.

Whiteout paused to mark several spaces in the ring, and a tall, powerfully built handler grabbed the lead. Whiteout sniffed his leg and peed on him.

The handler, though, hardly minding the toy breed in his arms, got down in Whiteout's face like a naughty canine's worst nightmare and positively growled, "*Nobody* pees on me, mister."

Whiteout whimpered and lay down like a penitent in the presence of the Divine and proceeded to lick his paws.

"You look at me when I'm talking to you, you bat-eared excuse for a mallie," the handler continued, and Whiteout's ears lay back and he lowered his head some more.

All Elijah could think was, *I want that dog. That dog wants to be my dog.*

Barbara appeared at that moment and gave a very convincing, "Oh, God, that damned dog."

Elijah found himself watching the resumption of the Yorkshire Terrier judging and the handsome handler's aplomb in returning to the matter at hand. His Yorkie was the judge's first pick.

Knowing he must find Paul and the red-haired groomer, Elijah started to turn away just as Sissy Atherton hurried to ringside, now leading a toy poodle. She spoke to Tall, Blond, Handsome and Authoritative-with-Dogs, then exchanged a quick kiss with him. Elijah noticed a rock the size of a shooting marble on her finger. *Ah, well.*

A deeper disappointment lodged in his gut, but he ignored it.

Just then, he saw Paul heading into the crowd and some other men—these in more conservative and predictable FBI dress—fanning out nearby, all of them following a handler in a buff-colored coat leading a handsome sable German shepherd dog.

"SOMEONE WILL DISPUTE IT," Clark said disinterestedly, walking away from the couple to whom he'd just presented a blue ribbon for their Yorkshire Terrier.

"Because you grabbed that malamute thing?" Like Clark, Sissy was reluctant to call the disobedient and goofy-looking animal an Alaskan malamute. "Where's Kennedy?" she asked. Her sister was holding Teddy aka Echo Springs Farm's Theodore, and Kennedy had promised to take him outside to be exercised before he went into the ring.

Sissy searched the heads for her sister, and what she saw alarmed her. Kennedy's blond hair looked wild, her face frantic, as she stood outside the restroom screaming at another woman and then began scanning the crowd.

Teddy was not with her.

Sissy felt only half a moment of nausea, of terror, before she, too, began searching the crowd.

Incredibly, she saw him.

Leaving the arena with a man in a buff-colored blazer. Without speaking to Clark, Sissy ran after the dog.

Handling dogs had made her accustomed to running in high heels. The thought of someone stealing Teddy—and she had no doubt that the man in the buff jacket was trying to steal her dog—electrified her.

She jostled a handler leading a Boxer, snapping, "That man's stealing my dog," and kept going.

Buff jacket was not looking back.

Outside, the heat and humidity enveloped her, but Sissy ignored them, streaking across the gravel lot filled with station wagons and the occasional Airstream trailer. She screamed, "Let go of that dog, you bastard! You are *not* taking my dog."

Buff jacket did glance back then.

Sissy was upon him, and yanked Teddy's leash from his hand. "You're a terrible person!" she yelled.

"Hey." He raised his hands as though to tell her to relax. "Calm down. I just wanted to find his owner. I'm glad you have him back."

"You're a liar," she said, shaking with terror for her dog. Then she heard the incredible—a growl, low in Teddy's throat. She'd never heard Teddy growl at a person in his life. "I'm going to call the police," she said, "and you're going to wait for them."

"No need for that," he said, backing away from her.

Sissy was torn. Only an evil person would steal a dog. But right now she must protect Teddy, which meant getting him away from this horrible individual. And although there were a few people in the lot, they seemed very far away from Sissy and the dog thief.

Until, abruptly, a sedan pulled up behind the man. He glanced behind him as men in suits got out of the car.

The handler with the Boxer appeared behind her.

She saw badges wink in the sun, heard one of the men say, "You are being arrested for the murder of…"

"Sissy?"

She wheeled around, unsure whom she expected to see. It wasn't Clark's voice.

And there, looking like a handler, stood Elijah Workman.

Her heart thumped. *Elijah.*

She jerked her attention free of him the same way she would correct a dog in obedience lessons—immediately and firmly. The dog thief was being arrested, and she abruptly remembered the horrible stories she'd heard of recent dog thefts; that was what might have happened to Teddy.

Her stomach revolted, and she spun away from the men and vomited on the hood of a nearby car.

"Sissy! Sissy!"

Clark. He was here.

"You're all right, Sissy. He didn't hurt you."

Another voice—yes, Elijah's voice—said, "She's not puking because she thought he'd hurt *her.*"

What a perceptive observation, was all she could think.

Clark passed her a clean handkerchief, and she dabbed at her mouth and her watering eyes, then crouched beside her dog, who had been whining and now licked her face.

She straightened up finally, half sagging against Clark, and turned to Elijah. "Clark, this is Elijah Workman. He's from Echo Springs. Elijah, this is my fiancé, Clark Treffinger-Hart."

ELIJAH HAD ALREADY DECIDED this was Sissy's fiancé, only his name had been a mystery.

However, introductions were interrupted by Elijah's need to speak with Paul to find out if any of the stolen dogs had survived. He knew, though, that the dogs were going to be a low priority for the FBI. The comfort was that they may have found their man and, if so, the creep would actually end up in jail. Seldom did animal cruelty prosecutions end so satisfactorily. In fact, he'd yet to see a case end that way.

When he was finally free to talk to Sissy, he saw Clark trying to persuade her to return inside, get out of the heat. That sounded like a good idea to Elijah, but she lingered.

"Elijah, I see you're working, but we're in town, and Mom and Dad are here. We'd love it if you'd join us tonight for a small party at Clark's club. It's to celebrate our engagement."

Clark's club. Ruefully Elijah remembered his own breakup with Sissy, still vivid to him. Well, she'd found someone right for her, Elijah supposed. "I'm not sure I'll be able—"

"Sissy, the man's obviously busy," said Clark, in the sort of voice a father might use with a teenage daughter.

Sissy seemed not to hear her fiancé. "Please," she said appealingly, her violet eyes searching Elijah's face, reaching into him. "It would be so great to have you."

"I'll…try."

Clark's club

"I STILL CAN'T BELIEVE you let a stranger watch Teddy," Mrs. Atherton said to Kennedy. "What were you thinking?"

"It was a *dog show*. There aren't bad people at dog shows," Kennedy exclaimed.

Elijah, eavesdropping from his spot by the punch bowl and table piled with shrimp and salads and any number of small delicacies, kept his eyes focused on Sissy's intended across the room. The small band playing the engagement party was taking a break, and Elijah was glad, not being in the mood for love songs of another era, an era that had ended just before the world was divided by the Vietnam War, by the suddenly clear reality of racism, by drugs and everything so different from what he'd known growing up. People protested actions he knew were wrong but also rejected those he believed were good.

Sissy seemed to be clinging hard to that older world, and Elijah was surprised—and not completely pleased— to see it.

Clark was an orthodontist—"But they met at a show!" Mrs. Atherton had exclaimed enthusiastically. "So we knew right away he was wonderful!"

Clark raised Norfolk Terriers.

"Of course they'll have shepherds, too!" Sissy's mother had continued to gush.

Clark certainly had straight, white teeth, Elijah reflected. At the party, Elijah had enjoyed talking with Mr. Atherton, but now he craved solitude. He longed to somehow free his mind of the horrors crawling through it: knowledge of the dogs stolen by the thief they'd apprehended that day, knowledge of what had happened to those dogs.

Not to mention the women who had been murdered. Sissy had been frightened for Teddy. Elijah—like Clark, he now acknowledged—had been frightened for her. But for Elijah, it had been fear with the knowledge of what the perpetrator could do.

Now he was glad he'd chosen the work he had rather than become a homicide detective or even remain a sheriff's deputy, glad his job didn't involve telling someone what ghastly act had befallen a beloved child or spouse.

To love animals and see them hurt was torture, yet he was good at this work. He saved animals, and the animals needed a voice. But how long could he keep doing it?

His whole life he'd wanted to be an animal behaviorist, even before he knew what one was. The Humane Society certainly gave him hands-on experience with animals; it was how he spent virtually all his free time. Watching animals. Trying to figure them out.

"He's a good man," said a voice beside him.

Elijah glanced over at Sissy, now dressed in an ivory suit. She was gazing in the same direction Elijah had been—at Clark Treffinger-Hart, who was talking with two of his former fraternity brothers.

"He seems very nice," Elijah agreed mildly. "And you have so much in common." He meant this sincerely, but even to his ears it sounded like a dig.

"In a way."

These didn't sound like the words of a woman avidly anticipating marriage. Elijah was reluctant to draw her out. The new Sissy was different from the old Sissy.

Primarily the new Sissy was unavailable. Soon she would be someone else's wife.

The *old* Sissy had been a little wild. Perhaps a shade of that woman was wondering if she wanted to be married at all, to anyone.

She wore her hair up in some kind of elaborate, elegant hairdo. It made her look very expensive. Her coltish adolescence had matured into beauty-queen poise. Even in heels she wasn't as tall as Elijah, but she came close.

"I don't like Norfolk Terriers," she finally admitted. "I'm not sure I can live with the yapping things."

Elijah threw back his head and gave a quiet laugh.

"It's not funny. I love dogs, but I don't love them all equally. I don't want to spend the rest of my life with all of them."

Elijah could not resist. "But you're in love with Clark. That won't be a problem."

Her silence lasted a little too long, and he thought she blushed. Then, abruptly she changed the subject. "Tell me what you're doing. You live here?"

"Right now I'm based here."

"And you're working for the Humane Society, investigating animal abuse cases. And you get paid for it."

"Very little," he admitted.

"It's probably because of me you're in that line of work," Sissy said.

Her ability to congratulate herself certainly hadn't lessened with the years. Sure, she'd introduced him to this kind of work, but she wasn't the reason he'd chosen to pursue it.

He supposed Ella was. And Lucky. Lucky had passed away three years before, and now Elijah only had one cat, Five, a polydactyl. He was going to look into adopting Whiteout, though. As he'd dressed for this party, he'd been able to smile because of the memory of the malamute's hot-dog-eating escapade. Whiteout would make him laugh, and he needed laughter.

Of course, he had to admit, even more often than his thoughts had turned to the malamute, they'd lingered in bemused admiration on Sissy

Atherton, giving a murderer what-for. *You're a terrible person.* It still made him smile. She'd nailed that one, all right.

Yes, she was the same Sissy he'd known.

He didn't want to think about it, about any of it. *I let her go.*

He'd let her go because he'd been sure that he didn't have what was required to hold her. For the first time he wondered if any man really did. She'd always been a bit willing to do the slightly dangerous, slightly unconventional thing.

He said, "So you're worried that your dislike of terriers is greater than your love for your fiancé?"

She sighed, apparently unwilling to admit that much. "My parents want me married, I'm a problem to them, you know. I studied theater at Sarah Lawrence, and they think I came home with funny ideas. Clark is their idea of the perfect son-in-law. I mean, we met at a show. What more could you ask for?"

"To meet in the German shepherd breeding ring?" Elijah suggested.

"Ha ha," she said mirthlessly, then shifted topics again. "So, are you married, Elijah?"

She must know he wasn't. No ring, for one thing. He shook his head.

"Girlfriend?"

Another shake of the head. His nerves were

thrumming faintly like guitar strings. "I'm thinking of getting a dog."

"Lucky's gone?"

He was touched she remembered the name of his pet. But it was because of Sissy that Lucky had survived. He told Sissy about Five, whom he believed to be an unusually intelligent feline. Then he confessed he was thinking of adopting the dog they'd used that day.

"What is it?"

"It's a malamute."

"Not that dog that got away and ran into the Yorkie ring? The one with airplane ears?"

"Yes," Elijah admitted. "What's wrong with him?"

Sissy made a slight face. "Well, I think *malamute* is a loose description. He looked like a mutt to me. I mean, I guess he's all right. You're not really into purebred dogs."

Elijah had to admit that he wasn't. "Not like Clark," he couldn't help murmuring.

She stared at him, and he thought she was going to make a snotty rebuttal. Instead, she again shifted the conversation away from her fiancé. "I've been writing plays. They've put on two of them in Echo Springs."

"Really?" Elijah tried to remember if he'd heard anything about this. His mother and the rest of his family still lived in Echo Springs, all but his brother Frank, who was in the army.

Sissy said, "That was a very bad man they caught today, wasn't it?"

"And a bad woman," Elijah agreed, because the dog thief's partner, the groomer, had also been apprehended.

"What did he do?" She sounded curious, but seemed to know what she might hear would be awful.

Elijah shook his head. "I don't want to talk about it."

"Maybe you can't," she said. "I mean, if it's confidential."

"It wasn't a nice case, Sissy."

"I didn't want to come here tonight," she admitted. "I just wanted to be with Teddy—he's at Clark's house with our other dogs. But Teddy doesn't know he almost got stolen."

"How did he get that name?"

"The whole litter was named for kinds of bears. Polar, Kodiak, Black, Panda, you know. Teddy was Theodore, and we thought we were going to sell him as a pet, but he's the best dog I've ever had." A moment later, she said, "It seems like your life's kind of lonely, Elijah."

He didn't know how to answer; she was right. He dated, but undercover work of any kind was stressful. He had become reclusive, and he never wanted to talk about the work.

He just wanted to save animals. As many as he could.

"I'm not sure I should get married," she whispered beside him.

He wasn't going to touch that one.

She clearly didn't expect him to. It was almost as though she'd been talking to herself, and she moved off a short time later.

Would she really marry Clark? Elijah had the strange feeling that if the orthodontist and Sissy actually married, Sissy's husband might find he'd gotten something more—something *else*—than what he'd bargained for.

As she walked away, an impish idea rose inside of him. The band leader was heading toward the stage, and Elijah crossed the floor to waylay him.

"Would you like to dedicate it to the couple?" the leader asked politely. He wore his black hair slicked back, a short, clipped mustache, and his singing reminded Elijah of a Latin Elvis Presley.

Elijah briefly considered this possibility. "Just say for the true romantics."

And as the man nodded with satisfaction and continued on his way, Elijah looked about for the Athertons to say good night.

June 4, 1969
Echo Springs

SISSY SAT on the upstairs balcony of her parents' house, just outside their bedroom, addressing a wedding invitation. Most of them had been sent out weeks before, but if she happened to run into an old friend…well, she couldn't *not* invite him.

She consulted an address on a cocktail napkin. *Elijah Workman.*

As she addressed Elijah's invitation, she reminded herself of all the reasons Clark was the right man for her. Not to mention the vaguely humiliating moment when she'd asked the band leader, "Did someone ask for that song?"

The Brylcreemed creep had looked a little too knowing when he said, "The tall, handsome gentleman… Ah, he is gone."

Yes, Clark was right for her, and she shouldn't wonder about Elijah's requesting "Let It Be Me," then leaving.

Sissy believed herself to be a passionate woman. While a student at Sarah Lawrence, she'd fallen for one of her professors and had begun a brief, tempestuous affair before learning from another student that he had a wife in Boston.

After that, she'd become careful. Around her, everybody in the country seemed to be going mad. Protesting the war, rioting, civil rights—it was so chaotic. She supposed that if it hadn't been for that one bad experience, she would be throwing herself into all of the insanity. Instead, she'd returned to the world of dogs, the security of the family kennel, life in Echo Springs and right into the sphere of someone like Clark Treffinger-Hart.

Why do I think of it that way? she wondered. *Why 'someone like Clark'?*

Because some suddenly sick part of her wondered if there were many men who would suffice, if he was simply a type who would fit the bill.

She remembered the days she had danced with Elijah to "Let It Be Me," the days she'd sung that song alone in her room like a prayer. He was the only one she'd really wanted. And she had never loved like that since.

The balcony overlooked the kennels. She watched Teddy and his brother Polar rush to the fence to bark at some birds.

This is crazy, Sissy. You don't want to marry Clark. You don't even want to be lovers with Clark.

Was that true? It couldn't be. She was attracted to Clark. He was handsome. Everyone said so. He believed her to be a virgin, and she'd never disabused him of the idea. She hadn't lied, of course, just never volunteered the mistake of her past. She knew if she'd told him, he'd have wanted to enjoy her charms; he'd have been unwilling to wait for the wedding.

So why was she making him wait?

Sissy stared at the name she'd scrawled on the envelope. If she were marrying Elijah Workman, would she make him wait?

But you're not marrying Elijah, Sissy dear.

Instead, Clark was driving down from Kansas City the coming weekend.

If you're going to marry him, Sissy...

Yes. Of course, she was willing to make love with him. Why had she ever hesitated? It was what they needed, what *she* needed to reassure herself, to go into this marriage full tilt, absolutely certain, the way she wanted to.

June 19, 1969
Cathedral of the Immaculate Conception,
Kansas City

Sissy stood in a tiny room off the vestibule, ready.

Dressed, at least.

Kennedy had perfected every last detail from seamed stockings and garter belt and tissue-delicate bra and panties to a dress nearly fit for the goddess Athena, a wreath of flowers for a veil over her long, straight hair. Yes, Sissy knew she looked spectacular.

But she was not ready.

She clung to Kennedy's hand on which sat a wedding band and engagement ring from the extremely suitable obstetrician, Gerry Fischer, with whom Kennedy was deliriously happy.

Her older sister's eyes focused on Sissy's as the mother of the bride entered the room. "Everyone's waiting, dear. Are you ready?"

Kennedy seemed to read the panic in Sissy's eyes. "Yes. Go sit down, Mother. That's your job right now."

"Sissy, we're all so happy for you."

But Heloise Atherton didn't sound happy. To Sissy's ears, she sounded threatening. Two days earlier, Sissy had dared to tell her mother she was having second thoughts about Clark.

Her mother had told her firmly that such feelings were natural and Sissy should ignore them.

Now Kennedy told their mother, "Mom, please go sit down. The procession can't begin while the mother of the bride is back here."

Sissy relaxed slightly. *Kennedy knows I'm freaked.*

With obvious reluctance and a phony embrace, her mother declared, "The next time I hug you,

you'll be Mrs. Clark Treffinger-Hart!" She then left the little room, failing to shut the door behind her.

Kennedy pushed it shut. "Are you all right?"

Sissy shook her head. "Kennedy, I can't do this." She wasn't going to tell her sister that three nights earlier she had made love—well, had sexual intercourse—with Clark in his room in the house where he'd grown up, creeping back to her guest room afterward. Last night she had stayed with Gerry and Kennedy in their big brick Colonial-style house so that Clark would not see her the morning of the wedding. Sissy had hated being intimate with Clark, feeling frozen, realizing the whole time she didn't want to be doing this. *I definitely don't want to do this for the rest of my life with this man.*

Kennedy gazed into Sissy's eyes. "You mean that, don't you?"

"Everyone's going to hate me. I'm so sorry!"

"No," Kennedy said. "You never will be." She embraced Sissy, still careful not to smudge their makeup. "Honey, I love Gerry to pieces, but marriage is just too hard to do with someone you *don't* love that much."

"Mom's going to die," Sissy said.

"Oh, she might try to kill *you*," Kennedy answered with a smile, "but she definitely won't die of this. If you ran off with Elijah Workman, *that* might kill her…."

Hairs rose all over Sissy's body. Along with the vision of somehow getting out of this wedding, she *had* entertained ideas of running off with Elijah. Truthfully she wouldn't give a damn if they were married. They could go raise Salukis in the Sahara desert for all she cared, but it would be exciting and fun, and she would feel free. Because nothing about Elijah belonged to the constraining world in which she now found herself a near-prisoner. "What makes you say that?" she asked Kennedy uneasily. *Let it be me.*

Kennedy gave her a sudden, sharp look. "I didn't mean anything. It's just Mom was falling over herself at the party at Clark's club to let Elijah know how completely taken you were, as though the fact it was an *engagement* party didn't really get the message across." Her eyes flashed away from possibilities she evidently decided were too disturbing to entertain.

"Look, honey. You wait right here. I'm going to find Jackie—" Clark's sister "—and tell her what's going on, then I'll be back to get you out of here. You can stay with Gerry and me till Mom's ready to be civil."

Sissy swallowed, thinking she would throw up if she received any more pressure at all from her mother to marry Clark. Kennedy left the room, shutting the door. The minute Jackie went up to speak to Clark and the priest, Sissy's mother would be out of her seat, hurrying back here. Kennedy would do everything she could to stop her, and Sissy pictured a pushing matching between her sister and mother in the cathedral's vestibule.

No... I can't stand this. I can't take any more....

THE CONGREGATION WAS RESTLESS. The wedding should have begun ten minutes earlier. Elijah, sitting on the bride's side of the church among people who probably earned in a month what he made in a year, had begun to suspect what he doubted anyone around him was suspecting.

These people, of course, didn't have the memory of Sissy standing feet from them at her own engagement party muttering things about Norfolk Terriers.

Elijah, who thought of terriers as ankle-biters, had, upon returning to his small rented house, consulted the AKC breed standards and been un-surprised to learn that while the temperament of the Norfolk Terrier merited one line (none of it actually offensive), the temperament of the truly unsurpassed German shepherd demanded half a page. He'd also read and bookmarked the entire section on Alaskan malamutes, ignoring anything in his new companion Whiteout that could be considered a physical fault because he didn't believe in such things.

The next morning, Whiteout, as though to emphasize that it was past time for Elijah to stop replaying everything Sissy had said of dogs and of doubts, destroyed the AKC book, depositing much of it in a newly dug hole in Elijah's tiny backyard.

Unaccountably, Elijah felt a spark of happiness and hope.

In all their years at school together, Sissy Atherton had never once been marked as tardy.

Now she was late for her wedding.

He watched the groom's sister hurry up the aisle in a blue bridesmaid's dress, and saw the groom's face fall.

He wondered if Sissy was on the premises and began concocting interesting scenarios. He imagined her running down the street in her wedding dress as he happened to be driving past— not in his third-hand Chevy Nomad but perhaps in a new Corvette. He wondered how rude it would be for him to squeeze out of his pew now, past the line of Sissy's society friends and relatives.

He did stand and say, "Excuse me," while the groom and his father conferred with the priest.

Sissy's immediate family were far ahead of him in the cathedral, and he hoped they would not notice him leaving. They didn't like him anyhow.

He genuflected, hurried back along a side aisle, past curious faces, dipped a hand in the holy water for a quick sign of the cross and passed into the vestibule. A bridesmaid and a groomsman stood in hushed conversation, glancing toward a closed door.

Well, he couldn't return to his seat now, and he knew with certainty that there would be no reason to do so. Instead, he walked out into the jungle sauna air and hurried to the old Nomad. The previous owner of the car had suffered a fender bender. Elijah and a friend had repaired the damage in the friend's body shop. It was a good car, excellent for transporting a malamute and going to the drive-in, but Whiteout was at home now, undoubtedly digging craters in the yard.

Clark Treffinger-Hart drove a Corvette.

Elijah rolled down the windows, started the car, turned it in the street and drove back toward the cathedral. He circled the block three times, slowing each time as he passed the front. What was happening inside?

Nobody came out.

Maybe he was wrong.

Later, Sissy would hear about his leaving and

wonder why he had walked out on the wedding. His mother would be appalled by his behavior. Fortunately his mother would probably never hear of it.

He made another pass of the church, certain his gut was wrong.

But just as the rear fender nearly passed the foot of the steps, he caught a glimpse of white from the corner of his eye. He braked and turned his head as white, flowing white, spilled out of the church. Not on the arm of the groom.

She was unaccompanied by a bridesmaid, though one stood in the doorway, making entreating gestures.

Elijah backed the Nomad to the base of the steps, and the bride raised her gaze. She lifted up her train and rushed down the stairs, and Elijah, feeling more exposed than he ever had in his life, could *not* let her open her own door, could not even reach across the front seat to open hers from the inside—his upbringing was too strong. He got out and hurried around the front of the idling vehicle to let her in.

Neither spoke while he tucked her in, folding the satin around her, draping the train in her lap, and closed the door. Sissy gazed at her bare left hand. She'd left her engagement ring in the dressing room.

Only after they'd driven away, when Elijah was stopped at the first light past the cathedral, did he break the silence. "Where do you want to go?"

Sissy tried to speak lightly, but her voice was husky. "I thought that was obvious. I'm running away with you."

CHAPTER FOUR

The first step in teaching a dog not to fight is preventing fights. If your bitch likes a scrap, never have her off-lead in a situation in which a fight could occur.
—*Teach Yourself, Teach Your Dog,* Elijah Workman, 1973

June 19, 1969

THE NEXT HOUR FLEW BY. Sissy had begged Elijah to take her to her sister's house, where the maid had let her in. While Elijah waited, she collected her car and some clothing and wrote a brief note to her family telling them she would be in touch. Then she asked Elijah if she could follow him to his house.

Soon, attired in bell-bottom jeans and a peasant blouse, she sat at his kitchen table with Five on her lap, while Whiteout paced around the table and Elijah. Sissy seemed content and utterly relaxed.

Elijah was not relaxed.

He suspected Sissy's fleeing her own wedding had been a good move, especially because of the things she'd told him, primarily, "Elijah, I'm just not in love with him." Nonetheless, he also felt a certain chaotic quality in her attraction to him. This must be what people meant by "on the rebound."

He didn't want to live with her without their being married. It would seem to justify her parents' disapproval of him years before. Besides, it wasn't what he wanted—not with Sissy. But of course, Sissy was just visiting, not sleeping with him—he'd made up the guest room.

He suspected, though, that it would take little more than a crook of his finger to get Sissy Atherton into bed with him. It was tempting, and he'd realized that when she'd entreated with him to let her stay at his house. They were past everything but caresses in a parked car. They were adults. He said, "I'm not sure that's such a good idea."

She counted Five's toes—extra toes that Elijah believed went with extra brain power—and said, as though the discussion had never ended, "See what a good idea it is to have me here, Elijah? Your animals need me. Probably some days you're gone all day, and they'll have me to keep them company."

"Sissy, we're not *married.*"

"Oh, don't be old-fashioned. Anyhow, you

have a guest room. Not that I need to sleep there," she added.

Elijah turned away.

"Not to put you on the spot or anything," she said.

He leaned against his refrigerator, his head against his arm, and kept his back to her. He wasn't shocked by what Sissy offered, but it jarred with some picture he carried of her—and of himself. "I don't want to do that to you."

At the table, stroking his cats, she looked at his broad-shouldered back uneasily. Did he believe her to be a virgin?

Sadly, she remembered her long disinclination to have sexual intercourse with Clark and her yielding at last to the impulse. And her professor before that…

Without turning, Elijah said, "You just ran out on your wedding. You can't think you want to marry me. You can't know."

Her chest seemed to swell with emotion. What if she told Elijah how she felt? He certainly wasn't the kind of man who would tell other people should he not return her feelings.

How can he return your feelings, Sissy? He hasn't seen you for years.

Yet there was something so much the *same* about Elijah, and she was, too, in so many ways the same as she'd been when they'd dated. At her core, she still knew him; he still knew her. "Oh, I'd marry you," she said. "You wouldn't try to make me be someone I'm not."

Elijah froze, his breath shallow.

She wants to marry me.

He wheeled around, sank into the chair next to hers and impulsively grabbed her hands. She was so intensely beautiful, her skin every cliché for white and flawless, her bones sharp and interesting, her mouth wide and inviting, her eyes such a deep blue they reminded him of violets. He gazed into those eyes and said, "Sissy, you're acting crazy because you got out of that wedding. I'd marry you in a heartbeat, but you don't know what you're doing. Your family doesn't want you to marry me. That might even be why you want to. They approved of Clark, and you don't love him. They don't approve of me, so..." He shrugged. "Do you hear what I'm saying?"

She nodded, and to his horror, he saw that she was crying.

"What is it?" he gasped. "What did I say? Sissy, I *like* you. I'm not saying I don't."

"And I like you—I always have. It was you who broke up with me, not the other way round."

"If I made love with you now—" his voice was unsteady "—even were to marry you, I'd feel like I was taking advantage of your vulnerability."

"Why does no one think I know my own mind?" she exclaimed, tears now running down her cheeks, washed free of makeup in his bathroom.

Impulsively Elijah reached for her, pulled her toward him and up into his lap. Her body felt so warm and taut and small, though she was a tall woman. He stroked her smooth straight hair, buried his face in it. She cried harder, shaking against him.

"You've had a bad time, haven't you?" he said, holding her more tightly, feeling her rear pressed against his legs, wanting her. *I can't stand this. I can't stand it. What am I going to do?*

She lifted her face, put her mouth near his.

Elijah yielded.

July 3, 1969
Echo Springs

THEY DROVE BACK to Echo Springs as newlyweds in Sissy's car, which was more reliable than Elijah's. He left Five in the care of his coworker Barbara, who hadn't stopped shaking her head since he'd requested her help earlier that day, asking her to follow them to the courthouse and act as a witness.

Elijah wished he and Sissy could have married in the Catholic church and hoped they could get a priest to bless their marriage at some point. Though he believed elopement was cowardly,

Sissy had said, "We're not eloping. We're both adults, and my parents have just paid for a big church wedding that I decided not to have. Let's just find a judge."

So they had. Unwilling to involve Kennedy, Sissy had accepted Barbara as witness, along with Elijah's friend Paul.

When they emerged from the courthouse after the brief ceremony, a policeman stood ready to hand Elijah a ticket for Whiteout's cratering of the flower bed beneath the window of the judge's chambers. Learning Elijah and Sissy were just married, the policemen tore up the ticket and suggested Elijah be more careful where he tied his dog in the future.

Now they were headed for Echo Springs, already driving slowly down the Strip to cross the dam. Determined that they would have a real honeymoon, Elijah had rented a small cabin for them on the Lake of the Ozarks—a good ten miles by boat from Sissy's parents' place and far less accessible by car.

Elijah dreaded Sissy's parents' reaction to their marriage. But for him, once they had become lovers, there was no going back.

He couldn't imagine what the rest of their life together would be like because he seemed to think about making love with Sissy twenty-four hours a day. She was the only woman he'd known so intimately, and he found her to be the most amazing creature he'd ever encountered. He supposed that on some level he worshipped her. In any event, he made every effort to treat her as though he did, especially when they were in bed. He thought he'd kissed, venerated, every part of her body, and he felt satisfaction that she wasn't so much his as part of him. They had truly become one person.

Despite his intense feelings for her, he wasn't looking forward to her parents' reaction. And he had other concerns. He didn't make much money with the Humane Society. Sissy wanted to teach Obedience in Kansas City, and Elijah agreed she would probably find plenty of students in the city, more than she could in Echo Springs, for instance. But they would still be poor, and he didn't think Sissy Atherton had ever been poor in her life.

Well, he would find additional work to earn more money. They'd be happy. And if he had to, he'd return to law enforcement.

Sissy's parents knew they were coming because Sissy had called from a pay phone north of Osage Beach. He'd heard her say, "Elijah and I are coming by. We have something to tell you." A pause, then, "Elijah Workman, of course. Who did you think I meant? The prophet?" Already getting snippy.

Elijah had tensed, not wanting Sissy to feud with her family, wanting them to be pleased by the marriage rather than offended by it.

Sissy seemed to have her mind on other things, though.

They were nearing the fudge shop and the dock, and she said, "Pull over!"

He did, into a conveniently vacated parking space. "You want chocolate this badly?"

"Not chocolate! We have to do this." She jumped out of the car, pulling Whiteout after her by his leash. Elijah followed her across the street to the fudge shop.

Outside, she put Whiteout's lead in his hand, then she pushed open the door. He saw her remonstrating with a teenager behind the counter.

A moment later, he saw her approach the jukebox.

Then he heard the opening strains from outside.

She rushed out, laughing, beautiful and giddy, kicking off her white high-heeled sandals and moving into his arms and singing with the words. He sang them back to her, sang of only and always and the greatest blessing of his life.

Sissy said, "We get to hear it three times."

Elijah threw back his head, laughing, and Whiteout jumped up on them both, kissing Sissy's face.

ELIJAH PARKED next to Sissy's mother's car outside the big white house with the kennels shaded by a canopy of trees. Sissy called, "Hi, Teddy! I missed you. Hi, China, sweetheart." Tossing the end of Whiteout's lead in Elijah's lap, she leaped out of the convertible and hurried across the grass toward the dog runs. The dogs seemed divided between ecstasy at the sight of her and sheer rage at Whiteout's presence.

Elijah cut the ignition, got out and glanced toward the front door as the screen opened.

Heloise Atherton stepped out, dressed in white slacks and a white sleeveless blouse, her hair up in French twist so rigid it seemed like a helmet. She said nothing, just glanced at Elijah and gazed under lowered eyebrows at her younger daughter.

Sissy looked up from petting one of the German shepherds to see her mother. She straightened and emerged from the kennel again, looking toward Elijah.

Elijah said, "Whiteout, stay. No chew." He shut the driver's door and joined his wife, and they walked up the steps together.

HE COULD COUNT on one hand the times he had been in the Athertons' living room. On the occasions he'd visited Sissy's house as her boyfriend, the room had rarely been used.

Mrs. Atherton said, "Would you like something to drink after your drive? I have lemonade." Her eyes had already taken in the slim wedding bands, and when Elijah saw her gaze, he wished he'd insisted on getting Sissy an engagement ring at the time they'd bought the wedding bands. But Sissy had said, "I'll always be taking it off, anyhow. We don't need it."

But he had bought her a heart-shaped iolite stone that hung on a gold chain because it was the same violet shade as her eyes, and Sissy loved it.

"I'm fine," Elijah said.

"Me, too." Sissy clung to his hand as she sank down on the couch. He sat beside her.

Her parents settled down, too, her mother on the very edge of a wingback chair, her father on a heavier chair opposite her.

"Elijah and I are married," Sissy said. "We're going to live in Kansas City. He works for the Humane Society, as you know, and I'm going to train dogs."

"Are you all right for money?" Mr. Atherton asked, actually quite compassionately.

"Yes," Elijah said quickly.

"When did all this happen?" Mrs. Atherton said in a determinedly uninvolved tone.

"This morning," Sissy replied, with a serene smile.

Her mother lifted her eyebrows thoughtfully.

Sissy realized she was digging her nails into Elijah's palm and stopped.

"Where have you been since June nineteenth?" her mother next asked in a slightly less neutral tone. "Living together?"

"Yes," Sissy said. "And now we're married."

Her father's jaw became quietly set. He simply nodded.

Heloise said, "Well, you've both got a long row to hoe."

Elijah realized that all his imaginings of this moment with the Athertons had fallen short of the unpleasant reality. To start with, they doubted he'd be able to take care of their daughter.

But he would. The Athertons had a different living standard than he did, but he and Sissy *would* have enough money.

Mr. Atherton stood up abruptly. "Well, I'm erecting a new toolshed. Would you like to see it, Elijah?"

It seemed an awkward suggestion, and Elijah remembered, in that moment, that the Athertons planned things in advance. Was Mr. Atherton arranging for his wife to be alone with Sissy? Elijah could hardly refuse.

"Thank you. I'd like to see it."

He squeezed Sissy's hand and looked at her to

make sure she would be all right. But she seemed undismayed by the turn of events, and was already glaring at her mother with fierce determination.

MR. ATHERTON SAID, "I think you should call me Alan."

"Thank you," Elijah answered.

Alan studied the newly erected toolshed, and Elijah stood beside him, also looking. Alan said, "Her mother's going to take this hard."

Elijah nodded. He didn't apologize for the way he and Sissy had done things.

"If I told you my concern," Sissy's father continued, "I'm not sure you'd believe me."

Elijah glanced up at his father-in-law's profile.

"I remember when you planned to attend university. I remember your curiosity about things, Elijah. And now—well, I can see that the university education just won't be possible. I don't like the situation for you because I know you to be capable of much more than you're doing."

Blinking, Elijah glanced at his father-in-law, then reached out and touched the toolshed, pretending to admire it, but thinking instead. Listening.

When Alan didn't continue, Elijah told him, "What I do for the Humane Society matters. I protect animals."

"Yes, but you have great curiosity, Elijah, and a good mind. I've never forgotten the way you observed our dogs, trying to find out what makes each animal tick, watching how they interact with one another. Myself, I imagined you might become an animal behaviorist, something like that."

Elijah flinched at his father-in-law's perceptiveness.

Alan Atherton turned, gazed at Elijah. They were the same height, perhaps Elijah a half inch taller. "I know you love Sissy, and I know you'll take care of her. But I hope it's worth it to you," he said, "and that it will never make you bitter."

The words were almost a malediction to Elijah. Bitter? Because he'd married the woman he loved? He found himself saying, "I certainly hope the same."

"DID HE GET YOU in trouble?" Mrs. Atherton demanded, using a curiously old-fashioned expression.

Sissy tossed her head indignantly. "Of course not. Elijah wouldn't do that."

"So this marriage hasn't been consummated," Mrs. Atherton clarified.

Sissy stood up from the couch. "I don't think that's any of your business."

Her mother rose, too. "I cannot believe you did this to us, not to mention Clark."

Sissy said nothing. It was time for her and Elijah to get going. Her heart twisted with the realization that this was probably the level of acceptance her husband could expect from her parents in the future.

At least Kennedy will be decent to him, she told herself, wanting to get back to Kansas City to tell her sister that she'd married Elijah.

"You know," Sissy said, "this family has always prided itself on being such a *good* family, but Elijah probably thinks he's married beneath himself. He has no idea we were so tacky."

"Beneath?" Mrs. Atherton exclaimed incredulously.

"We're going to go tell his mother next. I bet someone in that house will say congratulations."

"The Workmans have every reason to congratulate themselves on his ensnaring you. But rest assured, your father and I will protect any future inheritance of yours."

"Ensnaring me? You think he's a gold digger?" Sissy wanted to burst out laughing. Elijah was a man who loved to work, who liked *making,* not *taking,* money. "I've loved Elijah since I was about twelve. I'm *happy* to be married to him."

"That's only because you don't know what

marriage is. Marriage is like a long conversation, and you've decided to have it with someone who doesn't even speak the same language."

"So…you're not going to be civil to my husband."

"I'm always civil," her mother replied.

"Though we don't exactly have your blessing."

"Of course, you do," her mother answered. "You'll certainly need it."

Sissy took a breath. She had a plan. She'd come here with a plan. But for the first time she was afraid. "I've come home to get some things. And Teddy, of course."

Her mother stared. "Teddy is part of our kennel."

"I am his owner. My name is on his AKC registration." And she had earned some money—not much, but some—from his stud fees. Of course, now she herself wanted the best puppy he could produce.

"You're not thinking of breeding him in Kansas City, are you?"

Sissy decided not to answer. Teddy was *her* dog.

"Does Elijah even have a place to live? A yard? And what is that thing out in your car? I don't think either of you is ready for this."

Knowing how strongly her mother felt about

dogs, Sissy thought *this* referred to the possession of Teddy.

"You can't afford children," Heloise continued. "They'll have to be raised like the Workmans."

"I won't object to that," said Sissy. "I rather like the way Elijah has turned out."

Her mother sniffed. "I thought you were old enough to think of someone besides yourself, Sissy. But now you've gotten into this situation, and you're going to bring children into it, and you want to take Teddy, too. I can't let you do this."

Sissy had never been so angry in her life. She would not address further what her mother had said about children, which was so far beyond rude. Instead, she struck where she thought it might hurt most.

"Actually, Mom, you can't *not* let me. He's my dog."

"YOU'RE MARRIED?" Elijah's mother was a small woman, with dark hair worn in a severe and old-fashioned bun. Elijah had inherited her brown eyes.

At her feet, Teddy and Whiteout, who had determined they were friends, were sniffing the baseboards.

Mrs. Workman turned to Sissy, clasped her

hands and said, "Oh, I'm so glad. Oh, how lovely." Then, "But…" She looked toward Elijah.

Elijah knew what was coming. Matthew, the brother just below him in age, was in a Trappist monastery and they were expecting him to be ordained the following spring. "We'll speak to a priest, see if we can have the marriage blessed, Mom."

She still seemed uneasy, but nodded, willing to leave this detail to Elijah.

Elijah's teenage sister, Maureen, sat at the kitchen table in her waitress uniform, ready to go to work at one of the lakeside fish places. "Congratulations, Elijah. It's nice someone will have you."

Which earned her an ice cube down the back from Elijah's water glass.

Sissy felt accepted and was glad. She'd visited the immaculate but very simple house many times before when she and Elijah were teenagers. She liked the Workmans, though when they were all together, they made a crowd. She wasn't used to that.

Nervous, she watched Whiteout put his front feet up on the counter. She gave his leash a sharp jerk. "Off!"

Maureen said, "At least one of you will know what she's doing." And she gave Sissy a friendly wink.

Lake of the Ozarks

AN HOUR LATER, while Sissy and Elijah sat on the front deck of their honeymoon cabin, the dogs lay at their feet, each with a bone. The escape from Sissy's parents' house, had been made more unpleasant by the discovery, when they returned to the car, that Whiteout had jumped out and begun digging up her mother's rose bushes.

Then, there was her mother's fury at Sissy's taking Teddy, in the end the only way she could fully unleash her anger at her daughter's marriage.

Sissy moved to sit on Elijah's lounge with him. She grasped his closest hand, his left, with the ring that matched hers. "I don't have a wedding present for you."

"Or I for you," he said, pulling her against him. "This chair's not quite big enough for both of us."

"We'll just have to get closer. Okay, let's make a bargain. We'll each name a gift we want. And I won't ask for anything you can't give me, and I know you won't, either."

"Like making love five times a day?"

His warm eyes delved into hers, and Sissy couldn't help kissing him. "I love you," she said.

"I have everything I want," he told her, "but what is it you want?"

She sat up suddenly, urgently, and gazed at him.

"A kennel. I want to raise and show shepherds as my parents do. But I want it to be *our* kennel, yours and mine."

Elijah's heart sank. Sissy, who knew how expensive it was to show dogs in conformation, let alone to raise them, thought he could afford this. Even if he made enough money…

He thought uneasily of Barbara and of everyone else at the Humane Society. It briefly occurred to him that his job might actually be in jeopardy if he did this. Trying for tact, he said, "Wouldn't you rather stay with your parents' kennel? Show with them? Otherwise you'd be competing against them."

"I *want* to compete against them," Sissy answered, her voice fierce. "I want to meet my mother in the German shepherd ring, and I want to win."

Warily Elijah watched her eyes focus on some far-off victory.

"Don't you see, Elijah?" she said, turning to him. "She thinks I'm coming down in the world in every way, that even Teddy will suffer from our marriage. She wanted to breed me to Clark Treffinger-Hart—I know that sounds crass—but you're my choice, Elijah, and she said the most horrid things about the life we're going to have together. We have to have our own kennel, and by God it's going to leave hers in the dust."

Elijah met her eyes. "Sissy, you might be coming down in the world in some ways. I don't make that kind of money."

"But I have ideas. You see, *I'm* a really good handler. I can make money as one, as well as teach obedience. And I know how to do a lot of things myself. The grooming, for instance. Elijah, I want this so badly. I want to get to Westminster."

The Westminster Kennel Club Dog Show. Sissy wanted to go to the top. The top of her world.

And her world, in the view of the United States Humane Society, was one of questionable merit.

But Elijah didn't say that—wouldn't say that—not to this woman he loved. He would get flack for it, and he had no idea how they could pay for it, but how could he strike down her dream? "Okay," he said and kissed her. "We can try to start a kennel, in a small way. But not with the goal of hurting your parents. I don't want that."

"If you'd heard her, you wouldn't feel that way," Sissy replied.

But Elijah could imagine the kinds of things Heloise Atherton had said. What he felt was saddened; Sissy's mother couldn't like him or feel resigned to Sissy's having married him, yet he'd wished that she would. And he didn't intend to injure his relationship with her parents further. He said softly, "Yes, I would."

THEY MADE LOVE in the queen-size bed in the cabin's larger bedroom, and Elijah dispensed with condoms for the first time. "Oh, God," he whispered when he was inside her, when they were one. "Sissy…"

She looked at his face, the craggy, handsome face that kissed every part of her body, and his eyes were shining, wet with emotion. *He loves me. He really loves me.*

Her heart surged, too, and she tried to be closer to him. The intense pleasure he brought sought her out, vibrating through her, washing over her.

Sometime later, holding her carefully, Elijah said, "I feel like we've always belonged to each other. I think we were made for each other. Now I'm with you as I've always wanted to be, and I only want more. I want to be inside you to know what you think and feel."

Sissy pressed her face against his dark hair. "That's how I feel, too."

He met her eyes, and his seemed very beautiful to her. "You are so worth waiting for."

Sissy thought she knew what he was saying, that she had been his first. She touched his face, trying not to replay the question that had troubled her once before. Did he believe she had been a virgin when they'd first made love? He was so gentle, so careful never to hurt her.

She considered things she could say now. *I wish I'd waited for you.* But that wouldn't be quite true. If she hadn't slept with her professor, she might not have slept with Clark, might not have realized she didn't want to marry him, so might not be with Elijah now. One change anywhere along the line could have altered her life, and she was so grateful to be married to Elijah, in love with him. "I love you," she said.

But she didn't like his believing she'd had no other lovers. It hadn't bothered her for Clark to believe that, but she didn't want any misunderstanding or misperception between Elijah and herself. The problem was, if he carried that idea of her, it might be important to him. She didn't want to disappoint him with the truth.

She didn't want to risk his loving her less.

CHAPTER FIVE

After the incident with the babysitter and Gene's retreating to the kennel, from where our bitch Martha defended his sanctuary, it was my wife's opinion that Martha regarded our son, Gene, as one of her puppies.
—*Among the God Dogs,* Elijah Workman, 1990

July 20, 1969

SISSY SAT beside Elijah on the plaid couch that they both agreed was ugly yet extremely comfortable, and stared at the image of their planet on the television.

"God," Elijah whispered.

Sissy echoed the thought numbly. *God, don't let it be true.*

A man on the moon? No, not that. Many times in the years since she first left Echo Springs to go away to college she had felt her world turning upside down, but never so certainly as now.

She had everything she wanted in this moment. She was married to Elijah, who'd come home from work with shadows behind his eyes from what he'd seen. She'd discovered that she and the animals who shared the small house had the power to chase away those shadows. And they'd begun buying the house, which was small and tacky, but *theirs*. On top of all that, she had bred Teddy to two different bitches and was expecting a good show puppy from each breeding.

She had never expected this, though.

Her period should have begun three weeks earlier. She hadn't worried at first. She'd been late before, when life had become difficult, and she'd discovered to her horror that the man she'd been seeing was married. It had been exam week even. And certainly, running away from her own wedding counted as a difficult event.

She tried to work things out in her head, looked at the calendar a good deal, remembered the precise night she'd gone to Clark's bed. There'd been no concern about her becoming pregnant, not with their wedding just days away.

If she was pregnant, it *could* be Elijah's baby. It just wasn't very likely.

She was pretty sure she was pregnant. Her

breasts had changed, seemed to be changing each day.

It annoyed her that Elijah seemed to notice nothing. And it relieved her. The last thing she wanted was to appear worried. About anything. And she knew how Elijah would react to the simple news that she was pregnant—he'd be thrilled. He'd love her more than ever. It was part of his old-fashioned nature, a nature she found endearing, strangely at odds with his rugged, craggy good looks, the look his wolfish grin gave him.

And yet… And yet what a relief it would be to dispense with pretense, to say, "Elijah, I wasn't a virgin when I married you. I am not the embodiment of your romantic daydreams. I'm *human*." And flawed.

Well, he knew she wasn't perfect. He kept things tidier than she did. Never having lived in a home with servants, he and all his siblings had always been given household chores. She wasn't even an especially great cook, but he was in love with her anyhow.

Teddy jumped up on the couch beside her and began licking her face. She buried her fingers in the dog's fur.

The telephone rang, and she started to get up, but Elijah said, "I'll get it."

Sissy listened from the couch.

"Maureen? Well, hi."

Warmth filled his voice as he greeted his sister. "You're in Kansas City? How did you get up here? What?"

A long pause. "I'll come and get you."

Sissy stood up.

"It's Maureen," he said. "She's at the Crown Center."

Sissy looked at the clock on the wall.

Elijah was already grabbing the keys to the Nomad.

"I GOT A RIDE with the church group," Maureen said from the backseat.

Elijah knew it wasn't that simple.

"You know, there was a trip to the cathedral to hear this singing group."

"How did you get separated from them?"

"I didn't 'get separated.' I said I was going to stay with you. It's all right, isn't it, Elijah?"

Sitting behind the steering wheel, Elijah said, "Of course." And it hadn't been such an outrageous excursion—Maureen was eighteen. But he didn't think she should have been left alone at the Crown Center at this hour. "We were just watching the moon landing," he said.

"Right," Maureen said.

"We've put a man on the moon," he marveled.

"Yes," his sister said, distracted.

Sissy said, "I'll make up the guest room for you. It will just take a moment. Did you have any dinner?"

"Yes, yes."

SISSY HAD LEFT THEM ALONE in the living room with Teddy and Whiteout, and Elijah looked at his sister. She wore a long skirt with a white peasant blouse over it, her long, dark straight hair down. She was pale, though. "Elijah, please don't be angry and old-fashioned. I just had to get away. I have to tell someone. I don't know what I'm going to do. Well, I do know." She lifted her eyes, looked at him. "I'm pregnant."

Elijah sucked in his breath. His first reaction was outrage at whoever had let this happen to his sister. His second reaction was shock that Maureen had been intimate with someone. His third was that everything could be made right. "Who is the father?" he said.

"Just a guy." She shook her head. "No one who's going to marry me or anything. I met him at a concert in Jefferson City."

Elijah felt his mouth fall partway open.

"I'm going to have the baby. It will be all right. It's just…I haven't told Mom yet I just wanted— well, moral support."

No. She wanted *him* to break it to their mother. His hand in the ruff at Teddy's neck, the dog nuzzling his knee, he tried to think of something to say. Maureen worked. She lived at home with his mother, his other sister Jackie, who was two years younger than Maureen, and their youngest brother Adam, who was a year younger than Jackie. "What are you going to do?" he said. "Are you going to work and... Mom can't watch the baby while you work. She has a job, too." Then he realized getting frustrated wasn't useful.

"Okay," he said. "Everything will be okay." He managed a smile. "I'm going to be an uncle."

SISSY LAY IN BED beside him, feeling Elijah's alertness, his eyes staring at the ceiling. She knew he was thinking about his sister.

"It happens," Sissy said into the dark. "You know it does."

"I'm just...surprised. I never thought she'd do something like that. Meet a stranger at a concert and sleep with him that night. Do you know she doesn't even know his last name?"

This is your chance, Sissy. Say it now, for you and Maureen.

But knowing what she knew, that she might be carrying Clark's child, she couldn't.

"Shh," Sissy whispered. The walls were thin.

"Elijah, this is no time to sit in judgment of her, all right?"

"Is that what I'm doing?"

She didn't answer. Let him figure that one out for himself.

"I thought she was like the rest of us."

"The rest of who?" Sissy asked.

"My family, people we know, you and me."

She said, "I'm not as much like you as you seem to think."

A quiet pause. "You know what I mean," he said at last.

What Sissy knew was that he hadn't heard. Or didn't want to hear. It occurred to her that Elijah had never asked if he was her first lover. *He doesn't want to know.*

The realization freed her. She would behave as he was behaving. She would go to the doctor, learn if she really was pregnant, tell him, watch him be thrilled…

And never let him know that he wasn't the father?

The magnitude of the lie assailed her.

She pushed it away. No need to think about it now. Maybe she wasn't pregnant.

Maureen was, pregnant and unmarried. And Sissy was getting a clear picture of Elijah's opinion of that. The opinion that he—and Sissy— were people to whom such things didn't happen.

November 14, 1969

THE PUPPIES SISSY PICKED from the two breedings were a sable bitch named Martha with a very pretty face and a black-and-tan male called Acorn. At twelve and eleven weeks respectively, they were all ears and very busy. Elijah liked them, though Sissy felt the hesitation from him that she would expect from a different member of the Humane Society. She knew he had mixed feelings about breeding dogs, though he liked the animals themselves.

As predicted, he'd been delighted by the news she was pregnant. Her due date was March twelfth, and Sissy had opted not to enlighten Elijah to the possibility—nay, *probability*—that the child wasn't his. The suspicion clearly hadn't occurred to him; he was just happy they were having a baby and concerned for her health and happiness.

When she'd told her parents that she and Elijah were expecting a baby, her mother had said, "He'll want twelve, I imagine."

Sissy had retaliated by describing the two puppies she'd gotten out of Teddy from two different bitches. She took Teddy to a show in Jefferson City, and he beat her mother's dog Lionel, who hadn't yet finished. Of course, this wasn't the satisfaction Sissy wanted. Teddy had been bred by her parents.

It was a Friday morning when Acorn made

his first mistake, pooping in the living room. Elijah, knotting his tie, watched her rub the puppy's nose in the poop, saying, "No! Bad dog." She followed it up with a smack to his bottom.

Elijah said, "Just put him outside, Sissy."

"Oh, you think I'm supposed to do nothing when he poops inside?"

Elijah was often surprised by Sissy's primitive methods for training dogs. "I don't think what you just did is going to make any impression on him except that you're scary."

Sissy glared at him.

"He doesn't *want* to do that inside, Sissy. He's five feet from the door. He's a puppy. It was really my fault. I let him out of the crate, but didn't take him outside first thing. He's just a little guy."

Sissy stood rooted to the spot, staring down at the puppy, whose long tail was drooping. She looked at what he'd done to the carpet, then glared at Elijah. "Then *you* clean it up."

"Fine," he replied. "In exchange for one thing."

She eyed him warily.

"No hitting," he said. "Ever."

"How do you expect me to train dogs if—"

"I don't care," Elijah said. "My parents never hit me. I never hit Lucky, and I've never hit Whiteout. This is a rule being put down by your own personal representative of the U.S. Humane Society. No hitting. Live with it."

Sissy looked as though she wanted to smack *him*. Instead she said, "I don't agree with that rule."

"Then we're going to have a problem."

She glared at him and stalked from the room.

SHE WAS GLAD when he went to work that day. Elijah thought he knew so much about dogs, but *she* was an obedience trainer from a family of trainers. Her mother had gotten a score of 200 in Open with Ruby.

Sissy had to admit that when she got a dog to do what she wanted by force, part of her hated it, but they could make her so angry when they wouldn't listen. And she knew the bottom line of Elijah's morning edict—no one was going to hit their child, either. As though she would!

Their child... Sissy pushed that uncertain thought far away.

At the end of the day, as she was walking toward the bathroom, she discovered white paw prints on the dark green carpet. One set went into the bedroom, the other into the bathroom, where she found the cabinet door open and Martha standing in a white puddle. She looked up at Sissy, wagged her tail and sat down in the paint-like substance. Somehow, she or Acorn had un-screwed the lid from a bottle of shoe polish and dumped it out.

God, what a mess.

"Bad dog," she said sharply and instinctively reached out to smack Martha's bottom.

And stopped.

She remembered Elijah saying about Acorn, *He's just a little guy.*

She should have kept the puppies in their crates or in the yard or watched them.

Tears springing from her eyes, tears of exhaustion from the weight of worry about the paternity of the baby she carried, Sissy picked up Martha and carried her to her crate. Wiping her eyes, she shut the door and went to look for Acorn. He was lying on the bed, on a quilt liberally spotted with white footprints, beside Whiteout, who was licking his head. Teddy was outside in his run.

Sissy picked up Acorn and took him to his crate, which she'd lined with thick towels as she had Martha's.

The front door of the house opened, and Sissy went out to see Elijah come in pulling an animal on a lead.

At first Sissy didn't recognize it as a dog. Its head was shaved, the back sewn up. It was a white dog, and she thought it might be some kind of fighting breed, but it was small.

"Elijah, take it outside!" she exclaimed. "The puppies!"

They'd had long conversations about the need for him to maintain separate clothes to be worn in the filthy shelters he visited and helped shut down or reform. Eventually she would be breeding dogs in their house, and it was imperative not to bring home diseases that their kennel could catch.

"They bathed her at the vet."

"What's wrong with her? We don't need another dog." Then she saw his eyes and realized she'd spoken too fast and too angrily.

"Just German shepherd puppies?" he asked.

"God, what's wrong with the back of its head? Was it a dogfight?"

"She's from a laboratory," Elijah said, "and she's deaf, but she's probably getting the idea that she's not very welcome."

Indeed, the little dog was edging backward. The puppies cried in their crates, and Whiteout had arrived to see the newcomer. "Gentle, Whiteout," Elijah said.

"They might kill her," Sissy said frankly. "She's weak. That's how packs work."

She saw his eyes again, and he said, "Well, in

case our child should happen to be weak, let's start protecting the weaker members of the pack."

"How dare you?" she snapped. "Of course, our baby is going to be weak, and just who do you think is carrying our child? Who do you think is protecting this baby?"

Five had sensed the arrival of a new dog, but seemed totally uninterested in the arrival. Teddy, like Whiteout, had come for a sniff. Elijah said, "Sorry, Sissy. I shouldn't have said that."

"Thank you," she replied, clearly unmollified.

Elijah scooped up the small white dog. He hadn't meant to lash out at Sissy. The lab he'd visited that day had been very bad. He'd photographed dogs, cats and monkeys that had been abused, removed them to the shelter where most of them had to be put down.

Sissy came forward slowly, looked long at his face, then reached out for the white dog. "It's a puppy!" she said in outrage.

Elijah nodded. There had been others from the same litter—this was the only one that could be saved. He had taken her to the vet himself before coming home.

Sissy's slender hand reached up and touched Elijah's face, then she petted the puppy. She took her from his arms. One of the puppy's eyes was mostly closed.

"I think she's blind in that eye."

Sissy held back her feelings—wrath at people who could do this to an animal and at Elijah, who'd just had to bring this deaf and half-blind puppy home. Instead, she kissed the puppy's pink nose and said, "You have a wrinkly little face, don't you? I bet you're a smart girl." Actually, she didn't bet that at all, but if it was one things dogs had taught her—and, to give credit, Elijah had taught her, as well—it was the necessity of praise. "What are you going to call her?"

Elijah shrugged. "I don't know. I haven't… gotten that far."

"Well, I have a mess to clean up. The puppies dumped out white shoe polish and walked around the house."

Elijah couldn't help it. He laughed. Then he noticed Sissy's face. She'd been crying. Quickly he offered, "I'll clean the floor if you make dinner."

"Other way," Sissy suggested, frowning. She really hated to cook.

Elijah kissed her. "Want me to watch her? I didn't bring a crate for her."

"She can keep me company," Sissy said. "We have to start getting to know each other." She added acidly, "And I didn't hit Martha."

Elijah looked at her for a long moment. "Thank you. Thank you very much."

AS SHE SCRUBBED the carpet, she replayed the things Elijah had said, his protectiveness of weak things. Surely he would be protective of the baby, even if he learned it wasn't his? Surely he wouldn't reject her; he hadn't rejected Maureen, just seemed shocked by what she'd done. Maureen's baby was due the month before Sissy's, and both women were looking forward to the cousins being the same age.

Except they won't really be cousins.

Well, it would be just as though Elijah had adopted the baby. Except he wouldn't know that the baby wasn't biologically his.

I can't lie to him, Sissy thought.

The white puppy was not interested in exploring, seemed simply to want to stay right beside Sissy. She was probably terrified. Sissy gently stroked the silky head, avoiding the stitches and the one short, floppy silky ear. A man who brought this animal home would not hold it against her that…

She cringed at the thought of telling him. Now wasn't the time. When the baby was born, she'd see if it resembled Clark or Elijah, and then…

But should I wait that long?

Yes. If the baby was Clark's, the truth would make Elijah unhappy, and Sissy wouldn't put the worry into his head until she knew for certain.

She called toward the kitchen, "How about Belle? It means beautiful."

He didn't respond. Instead, she heard his footsteps, and a moment later he stood in the doorway and she heard the stereo in the next room. He pulled her to her feet, gazing down into her eyes.

Her heart thudded, and she wondered at the goodness of a God who had given her this man, who was so in love with her, taking her in his arms to dance with her on a shoe-polish-mottled carpet where a deaf and blind puppy sat waiting trustingly.

She lifted her lips to his, kissing him back, and when that song, their song, ended, he crouched down beside her and the puppy.

"Belle," Sissy repeated to the dog. "I wonder if she can hear at all."

"If not," Elijah said, "I think she'll learn to read everyone's vibration—you know, the way our footsteps feel."

"I suppose that makes sense," Sissy said. "And of course, she can smell us. But I don't know how I'm going to teach her anything, especially if she can't see."

"We'll figure out how," Elijah said. "She'll teach us."

Sissy gazed at Belle, knowing he was right.

"Think what an accomplishment it will be,"

Elijah pointed out. "You'll be the Annie Sullivan of dog trainers."

Sissy knew he was thinking of Helen Keller's teacher. Finally she whispered, "If only I could be."

Elijah knelt beside her, grabbing her hands. "You can, Sissy. You can do anything."

Everything, she thought, *but tell you that this baby might not be yours.*

CHAPTER SIX

We are not wolves, and neither are dogs. To roll a dog on his back and growl at him is only an approximation of canine communication. And what it teaches the dog is questionable. The essence of good obedience training is to help dogs want to make the choices you want them to make because it's best for them.

—*Crossover Language,* Elijah Workman, 1988

March 11, 1970

"I THINK HE takes after you," Elijah said, smiling.

Sissy drew in a breath, looking at her son cradled against her breast. The child had been born with fair hair, with eyes an indeterminate shape. Sissy had sworn that at this moment, on this day, she would tell Elijah the truth, if this baby was not biologically his.

How could you tell with a baby?

The baby had a very distinctive chin, which had Clark Treffinger-Hart written all over it. "*I* want him to take after you." And that would never be. In addition to that chin, the baby had other, even more distinctive features of Clark's. First, a characteristic dip in each shoulder blade. Second, hair on his shoulders. Clark was blond but very hairy. Sissy remembered once hearing a newborn resembled its father so that he would recognize and protect the child. This was Clark's child.

And Elijah was clearly ignorant of that child-birth lore.

He smiled and kissed her, and she lifted her eyes to his.

I can't tell him.

The truth would only make him unhappy.

Kennedy and Gerry had been in and out, admiring the baby, congratulating both of them. Sissy had been tempted many times during her pregnancy to bring the question of what to tell Elijah to her sister, but she'd always stopped herself. Either it would be her secret to carry alone, or she would tell Elijah.

She looked at him, wondering if the truth really would be cruel, if it would be the better part of valor to keep it to herself.

There was the question of inherited family conditions, but Sissy knew of nothing major in Clark's family.

What she wanted in her heart was to tell Elijah, to hear him say it was all right, to say that he would love the baby as his own. She wanted to give him the chance to do all those things.

I must, she thought.

He said, "Ezra James?"

Sissy had liked the sound of Ezra Workman; the name was her choice. Elijah, who'd been less keen, had suggested they give their child a name he wouldn't hate them for later. But Sissy had said, *I like Ezra! He's a prophet, like Elijah.* Now, she said, "His name means 'help.'"

"If only James meant 'his parents get rich,'" Elijah replied.

They both laughed, and he hugged her and the baby. "May I hold our son?"

In that moment, she decided. Ezra Workman was Elijah Workman's son, and that would be the end of the matter. Yes, she'd be more comfortable if she could tell him the truth and if Elijah would accept it and love her and Ezra to the same degree. But that was too much to expect—from a man like Elijah anyhow, a man who'd saved himself for her. This would be better for everyone. For her, for Ezra, for Elijah.

THAT EVENING, Elijah walked with Ezra in the hall outside Sissy's hospital room. His mother, Maureen and her new baby Ashley, and his brother Paul had all come to Kansas City to see Ezra. To Elijah's disgust—and pain for Sissy—the Athertons had not. Instead, Heloise Atherton, with more travel resources than anyone in the Workman family, had said, "Well, we'll look forward to seeing her next time you're down here."

Her husband had cleared his throat but had not argued.

Now Elijah wondered whether Mrs. Atherton would have been up to Kansas City like a flash if the baby had been Sissy's and Clark's. He knew the answer. Heloise's coldness was directed at him.

God, their first grandchild, and they didn't want to see him as soon as possible? Elijah wondered if, hoped that, at least Alan would break away and come up to see the baby.

Ezra was a beautiful baby, at least Elijah thought so. He marveled at his perfect tiny fingernails, at the smell of him. He didn't think he'd ever smelled anything truly new before. To his eyes, Ezra looked like Sissy. He thought the nose would be Sissy's, straight and narrow and elegant. He didn't see the Workmans' trademark bump, which made his family's noses so hawklike.

As he wandered the corridors with his infant

child, nodding to an occasional passerby who smiled at the new father he was, his chest filled with pride. *My son.* He didn't dream of Little League and football games. He just knew himself to be in love with his child, proud of him, wanting everything good for him.

A door ahead of him swung open, and a tall figure strode in, looking about, and instantly spotted Elijah. A bright smile broke over Alan Atherton's face and was mirrored in Elijah's.

Alan hurried toward him. "Is that my grandson?"

"HEY, SISSY." Elijah spoke softly from the doorway. Sissy looked up, her arms already reaching for Ezra, which made Elijah's heart swell with love for her. "You've got another visitor."

She saw her father, and her eyes instantly welled up. She lifted a graceful white hand, trying to stop the tears, but her father came to her bedside and embraced her. He said, "This Ezra of ours is the handsomest child I've ever seen. And lucky in his parents."

Unexpectedly, Sissy sobbed against her father's chest.

Alan said, "Your mother's afraid she's coming down with something, or she would have been here. She didn't want to risk giving it to Ezra, but she insisted I come. Not that she had to twist my arm too hard."

The lie was smooth, and Elijah breathed some relief, seeing that Sissy, who hadn't heard her mother's voice on the phone, had bought it. Of course she wanted her parents to see Ezra. Even more, she must have wanted *them* to want to see him. Elijah pushed aside his own anger at her mother's cruelty. He hoped instead that Alan's news about her pending cold *was* true, though Heloise hadn't mentioned it earlier.

It was past visiting hours, but Elijah had spoken to one of the nurses, and she'd said, "Just be very quiet. It will be fine. I dare say it's good for everyone."

Elijah had thanked her heartily and reminded himself to tell her supervisor later what a fine nurse she was.

After Mr. Atherton left and Ezra slept in a bassinet beside Sissy—a forward-thinking practice when many hospitals still separated mother and child during many of the hours after birth—Elijah looked into Sissy's eyes and said, "I thought the day we were married was the happiest I'd ever known. But this day tops it."

He saw her swallow, and thought for a minute that she might cry again. "Are you all right?"

She nodded with a tremulous smile. "Completely."

June 21, 1970
Echo Springs, Missouri

KENNEDY WAS EXPECTING her first child, and Heloise Atherton spoke of that as she sat with Sissy in the Atherton's kitchen, holding Ezra. She told Sissy, "They're registered at Neiman Marcus, of course. Kennedy threw that shower for you, so you have some things for your baby."

Sissy wanted to snatch Ezra back from her mother. As though sensing this, her son began to fuss, and Sissy felt her breasts start to leak. She took Ezra to feed him, and her mother said, "It's good you're nursing. It will keep you from getting pregnant again first thing. I suppose he doesn't believe in birth control."

Thinking of Elijah, Sissy wanted to cry. Birth control? She *longed* to have Elijah's baby. She loved Ezra totally, would have changed nothing about him, yet there was something wrong in her marriage and it was the lie of Ezra's paternity, which could only be right when she bore Elijah's child. That, she told herself, would fix everything between them. And really, she was the only one who felt that way, because Elijah was perfectly happy. From his point of view, she'd given birth to his son, and their lives were perfect.

From her point of view, though, a lie was all that kept her from losing his love.

Sissy actually felt tears fall from her eyes as Ezra latched on to her nipple. She glared at her mother. "Why do you hate him?"

"Hate him? I certainly don't hate him. He's your husband. He's part of the family now."

Sissy heard this as, *He's part of the family now, and there's nothing I can do about it.* "You say mean things about him."

"Of course I don't, Sissy. He's the person you chose. He doesn't know the people we do. He's different, but he's your husband."

Sissy thought of Martha at home, of Martha who was such a perfect puppy. When she was three or four, Sissy would breed her to a dog of her choosing. Sissy was still thinking of names for her kennel. The kennel that would show this bitch across from her the truth about breeding.

She said, "I'm beginning to think I'm different, too."

"Of course you're not. You're our daughter," her mother said simply.

Sissy tried to imagine how her mother had come to be the way she was. Why did class *matter* to her so much? Her mother was from Boston and spoke of her debut there. She and Sissy's father had met at a dog show. He was breeding golden retrievers at the time, but easily switched to shepherds.

"What does he do for the Humane Society?" Heloise asked. "Tell people they shouldn't have pets?"

Sissy stood, still nursing, and tried to grab up Ezra's diaper bag. The zipper wouldn't close all the way, so it gaped.

Her mother said, "You really should have something better."

Sissy, crying, knew her mother wasn't talking about the diaper bag. She looked her mother in the face and said, "You're making me hate you. I love Elijah. Please stop doing this."

Her mother saw her tears. "Honey, don't over-react."

Through a face that felt as though it was falling apart, Sissy managed to show her teeth as she left.

July 3, 1970

THEIR FIRST WEDDING ANNIVERSARY fell on a Friday, and Sissy didn't really expect Elijah to remember. If he did, she wasn't sure what she would feel. The lie between them, the lie she swore to keep till death, was changing her in ways she hadn't anticipated. She felt that she'd been granted the greatest of life's graces and had destroyed it somehow.

But how could she have come out of it all right?

If she hadn't made love with Clark before the wedding, she might have actually married him. And if she told Elijah that Ezra wasn't his son, it would hurt him. It might destroy him.

Elijah came in the door at six to find her perfecting Belle's heel by holding a treat next to her own calf as they walked back and forth across the living room. Belle knew how to heel, had learned quickly, but Sissy was constantly in search of the stop-on-a-dime automatic sits she was used to seeing in the obedience ring.

Sissy glanced up and saw the flowers in Elijah's arms. It wasn't the traditional bouquet of red roses but a potted orchid.

"Happy anniversary," he said.

"It's beautiful." Sissy had always loved orchids, and Elijah had bought her an orchid corsage for the one formal dance to which he'd taken her when they were in high school.

"I got you a present, too. I guess you got the kennel last year," he said, referring to his okaying her plan on their wedding night, "so I thought I should keep up the dog tradition."

He handed her a small white leather change purse shaped like a dog's bone.

Sissy laughed, reached up and kissed his mouth, clutching the purse in her hand.

She turned toward the stereo. "We have to dance!"

He said, "Aren't you going to look in it?"

Sissy looked at the purse in surprise. They were so careful with money. She had made Elijah a card. She'd been trying to knit him a sweater for some time, but it wasn't going very well. With luck, it would be done by winter time.

Carefully Sissy unzipped the bag. Inside was something small wrapped in white tissue paper.

"I have the box," he said.

It was a ring, a sapphire eternity ring.

"They're the color of your eyes," he said. "And there's no stone to stick out and catch on things."

Sissy's eyes flooded, and she wished for something that would cost no money, that she could tell him the truth about Ezra and that he would love her as much as he loved her now. She held out the ring and offered him her left hand so that only he could remove the wedding ring and slide it back on after the sapphires.

He said, "Is it all right?"

She clung to him, then heard Ezra's soft cry from the next room. "It's perfect," she lied. The ring was perfect; it was their marriage that no longer was.

March 14, 1971
Kansas City

SISSY EMERGED from the obstetrician's office into morning sunlight, Ezra toddling beside her, holding her hand. *Yes!* She was pregnant. Elijah's baby. Now, when Elijah made love to her, she could feel as though it was really for her, not as though she must inhabit some other place for fear of his seeing into her mind. She was in love with Elijah, and to all appearances, he was mad about her.

But it's not real. He can't really love me because I'm not who he thinks I am.

Strangely she both resented this and deeply feared Elijah's learning the truth. She truly wanted his love, even if it was his love of a shell he believed to be her.

But with another baby, a baby that was his biologically, she would become the person he thought she was. Right? He couldn't not love her after she'd *actually* borne his child.

At work, Elijah was still investigating the abuse of animals in research labs. He made frequent trips to Washington to testify before Congress on behalf of animals. Sissy appreciated what he was doing, but disliked the people he worked with because she bred German shepherds, and the people at the Humane Society never hesitated to butt in and say it was a terrible thing to do.

Which simply wasn't true.

But she recognized how careful Elijah was never to criticize her for what she did, and to be as much a part of the kennel as he could be, even working with the dogs in obedience, using his own methods, which sometimes had phenomenal results. He'd told her, "I try to figure out each dog's strongest drive and use that in training. Martha isn't that interested in food. She loves praise." Drives? Yes, well, Sissy had almost broken her ankle thanks to the results of Whiteout's favorite drive—digging.

Elijah told her, "There is no *digging* drive. He's a malamute. Digging is just something he does."

Sissy had traded stud services from Teddy plus money she had made teaching obedience to acquire a wonderful black-and-tan bitch named Julia. Julia was expecting her first litter in five days.

Sissy had tried to involve Elijah in selecting a name for the kennel, but he offered no suggestions. Sissy badly wanted his input. Her father was every bit as involved in showing dogs as her mother was, and she still hoped Elijah would be the same way.

Outside the doctor's office, Ezra said, "Park?"

"Yes," Sissy answered, smiling at him. "Yes. That's where we're going. And then we have to go home and take care of the dogs."

SHE HAD PLANNED a romantic announcement of her pregnancy. Instead, Julia began first digging in the yard, then in the laundry, whining, pacing, anxious.

Sissy took her to the whelping box. "Ezra, you need to be a good boy. Julia's having her puppies."

Ezra came into the "puppy room" which was actually the little house's side mudroom, with his blanket. He sat on the floor, watching with concern as Julia began shaking her towel. Sissy tried to explain. "She doesn't know what's happening, and having puppies hurts a bit. But it will be okay. Some kinds of hurt are normal, and this is one of them."

Soon Sissy's attention was divided between Julia, each new puppy—removing the sac and searching for a sound or sign that the puppies were breathing and weighing the newborns and recording their weight—and Ezra, who was disinclined to go to sleep.

Elijah was late getting home from work, not returning until eight-thirty, by which time Ezra had fallen asleep in the corner of the puppy room. So far Julia had birthed five puppies, one sable female, two black-and-tan females and two black-and-tan males. Elijah found Sissy catching another puppy and drawing the sac from it. A sable male. Elijah sank down beside her on the floor, pulling off his blazer and tossing it behind him.

Julia half-sat, half-squatted, turning and turning around, and another puppy was born into Sissy's hands.

"I'm pregnant," Sissy said.

Elijah leaned forward to see around her long hair, which had darkened to a light brown-sugar color. She smiled her wide, beautiful smile at him.

He grinned broadly and hugged her, then asked, "Is everything all right?" He glanced at their sleeping toddler.

"Yes," she said quickly. Sissy was distracted, not so much by Julia's labor and the new puppies but by the anticipation that now everything between her and Elijah would feel *right* to her. And it did not. The baby she carried was his, but the lie around Ezra remained. She tried to cover her preoccupation. "I still don't have a kennel name, and I have puppies to register."

Elijah watched her. There was something else, he knew, something she wasn't saying. He stood and picked up Ezra to take him to bed.

He returned in minutes. "What is it?" he said.

The temptation came to her again, the temptation to confess all. Discretion was not, after all, the better part of valor; it was cowardice. She now knew that what she most feared was not Elijah's anger or the loss of his love—it was his pain. She did not want to hurt him. She pretended again, watching Julia, uttering a truth that was not *the* truth. "I wish you wanted to be more a part of this. The kennel, I mean."

They sat in silence for a while. Elijah studied Julia as she labored, watched the birth of the next puppy. He watched Sissy catch it, and begin to care for it. He said, "Tell me ideas you have for kennel names."

But Sissy was rubbing the puppy vigorously, then suctioning her nose and mouth with a bulb syringe. "Come on, baby, wake up."

Then a small sound from the puppy.

"Good girl," Sissy whispered. Minutes later, as she weighed the puppy and recorded the number, she answered Elijah. "I wanted to combine our names, like Elisis or something."

He laughed. "It sounds like bad Latin."

"How about E.S.?" Sissy asked.

Elijah thought he knew what lay beneath the question. She wanted to be thoroughly united with him through the kennel. The knowledge touched him, and he was ashamed that unconsciously he must have been distancing himself from the breeding of dogs, being more Humane Society rep than Sissy's husband.

"How about something from mythology?" he suggested.

"I can't think of too many positive dog images

from mythology," Sissy admitted, half relieved he seemed to be accepting the supposed source of her discontent. Another part wished he would keep probing for the real truth, until it *must* be told.

But Elijah was thinking of Ezra and of the child Sissy carried and of the fact that he would do anything for this woman, anything of which he was capable, when he whispered, "Genesis. Beginning. And it has *genes* and *Sis* in there."

Genes. The mention of the word stopped her. But he couldn't mean anything, except in reference to the genetic characteristics of their dogs. Sissy blinked up at him. "It has a couple of Es as well. I like it."

He smiled and touched her abdomen lovingly, reverently. "But I still have to confess, I'm more excited about Genesis's second child."

With a miserable shiver, Sissy tried to recall whether Genesis's second-born had been Abel or Cain.

CHAPTER SEVEN

When we came home, there were no puppies
and no Julia in the puppy room. It took us ten
minutes to find them in the hamper where
Julia had moved them.
—*Dog Brethren,* Elijah Workman, 1977

October 6, 1973
Greenwich, Connecticut

ON HIS SON Gene's second birthday, Elijah found
himself standing next to Clark Treffinger-Hart at
a dog show. Sissy was in the ring, handling Martha
against a bitch from Echo Springs Farm German
Shepherd Dogs among others, and she had sent
Elijah with the two boys to buy more bait, which
was allowed in the breed ring. Usually they
brought their own in a large cooler, but they were
so far from home at this show. They had brought
two cars so that they could show the four dogs that
they'd entered. Sissy talked about their buying a

trailer—perhaps an Airstream—but Elijah wasn't sure where the money would come from. Sissy helped finance showing dogs by handling other peoples' animals in the breed ring, and Elijah had learned how to do the same.

He learned what was important to the dogs by watching them, learning from them. They often liked one another's company, but Belle, their blind and deaf dog, preferred people. Elijah kept trying to learn what they wanted, and he recorded his discoveries, writing about the dogs. The contrast between watching them when they were happy, when they were in their element, and seeing what he did in his work, opened the door to new ways of seeing animal behavior. To Sissy's surprise, he'd actually sold an article entitled "Drive Discovery: Learning What Your Dog Wants and Making It Work for You" to the leading dog-training quarterly.

He looked thoughtfully at Clark Treffinger-Hart.

Sissy's former fiancé was as handsome as when Elijah had first seen him, but Elijah felt no jealousy. The past was past. He doubted Clark would recognize him, but the other man did turn around and glance at the two boys, Ezra with his curly blond hair and light aqua-blue eyes, which were a bit like Alan Atherton's, and Gene, who looked, said everyone, like Elijah. Clark seemed to do a double take on Ezra, then looked up at Elijah and nodded.

Elijah smiled back. He held three-year-old Ezra by the hand and Gene in his arms. He wasn't sure Clark recognized him when the handler turned back to the counter to buy dog treats from the vendor.

Elijah realized he was holding his breath. Ezra said, "Dad? Can we buy dog toys?"

Clark turned around and seemed to examine the children again, probably startled to hear perfect enunciation from a three year old.

"Not right now."

Elijah decided not to reintroduce himself to Clark.

The vendor counted Clark's change, then the other man walked away, looking prosperous in his light tan blazer, tie and creased trousers, ready for the breed ring.

Elijah, who wouldn't be taking any dogs into the ring that day, wore jeans and a flannel shirt.

Ezra's small hand tugged at his as he set his treats on the counter, preparing to pay the vendor. "Dad," he said again, "are we going back to watch Mother in the ring?"

"We are," he said, and touched Ezra's blond curls. For a strange moment, the memory of

Clark's face seemed to blend into Ezra's. Elijah blinked and thought nothing of it.

"YOU LOOK just like your dad," Alan Atherton said, holding baby Gene. "And a handsome fellow you will be. I think I have the best-looking grandchildren anywhere."

Elijah scooped up Ezra. Ezra said, "Can we go see the Akitas?" At present, Akitas were Ezra's favorite breed. There were rarely many of them at a show, but so far Ezra had counted five at this one.

Sissy heard him and murmured, "Yes. Sure."

She was reasonably content because although Martha had not won, she'd placed ahead of ESFGSD's China Daughter. The judge had told Sissy, "She really has a beautiful face. She's a lovely bitch."

Unfortunately Clark was at this show. That troubled Sissy because to her it didn't seem out of the realm of possibility that someday Elijah would notice that Ezra resembled Clark.

Also, she disliked spending time near her mother, who was rude to Elijah. Not only that, but Sissy had noticed the tension between her parents over this fact, their differing opinions of Elijah. Sissy loved her father and didn't want his life to be miserable. But when it came to Elijah, Heloise might do her best to make it so.

Heloise Atherton surveyed her husband and family, including Kennedy and Kennedy's daughter, Ellen. She said, "Ellen, you're a lovely girl, aren't you? Here, Kennedy, let me take her."

They traded a leash attached to China Daughter for a child.

Sissy had Martha in a sit stay, which the sable was maintaining nicely.

Elijah saw China Daughter's lip curl, and he grabbed the leash from Kennedy, pulling the bitch back just as she went for Martha.

Heloise screamed, "What are you doing?" and pushed the baby back at Kennedy to grab the leash.

But Elijah had made the correction, Sissy had pulled Martha out of reach and the incident was over.

"What did you do to her?" Sissy's mother demanded.

Ezra said, "China Daughter curled her lip at Martha and tried to bite her."

Heloise stared at her grandson. "Ezra, my dogs don't fight."

Elijah was outraged on Ezra's behalf.

Ezra replied matter-of-factly, "Well, she *tried* to, but my dad stopped her."

Heloise glared at Martha, then told Sissy, "You better hope the judge didn't see that."

As though Martha had started it.

Sissy rolled her eyes. "Elijah, I need to put Martha away."

Alan said, "Gene and I will come with you."

His wife said, "Sissy, denial is no way to raise dogs. I hope you do better with your children, at least. Though I'm doubtful." She cast a disparaging look at Ezra.

Elijah turned away with Ezra and strode toward the Akitas, Sissy trailing after with her father. Elijah heard her hiss, "I'm not speaking to her anymore, Dad, until she learns to be civil to my family."

"You know she's had health problems, Sissy."

The health problems were mental health problems, but no one said it. Heloise had spent some time in a hospital earlier in the fall but seemed unchanged to Elijah. He'd resisted ever saying what Sissy had voiced at one point: "Maybe they can give her medicine to make her act like a human being."

"Health problems are no excuse for being mean, especially to a child. And Ezra was right. Martha didn't so much as growl, and I heard China Daughter begin to snarl. For Mother to act that way to her own grandchild…"

Elijah hurried ahead and looked at Ezra's face. He told his son, "You were right. I saw China Daughter's nose wrinkle, too. Your grandmother was looking at baby Ellen and didn't see."

Around his very light aqua eyes, Ezra's long lashes and lush eyebrows were a shade darker than his hair. He was cherubic, the kind of child whom women stared at in wonder. Elijah was secretly pleased that Ezra seemed to disdain this sort of attention. "Why doesn't Grandma like us?" Ezra asked.

Elijah wasn't sure what to say. It wasn't in him to lie to Ezra, but nor would he criticize his son's grandparents. "I think she's not very happy. Sometimes when people aren't happy they find reasons not to like other people. It's nothing to do with you, Ezra. It's all to do with her."

Ezra exclaimed, "There are the Akitas!" and squirmed to be let down.

As Elijah set him on his feet, he heard Sissy and her father still behind them, Sissy saying, "And this stuff about Clark and Berkeley. Like after four years of marriage and two children I'm going to break down sobbing at the news."

Elijah turned around, taking a quick glance back at Ezra, who had sat down at the edge of the ring where the Akitas were being shown. "What's this?"

Sissy's gesture with her nonleash hand was meant to convey the triviality of the subject. "Oh. Clark's engaged."

"Really," said Elijah without much interest, eyes on Ezra. "Who's he marrying?"

"Berkeley Ludlow. She handles sporting breeds and she's in pointers."

"An excellent handler," Alan put in. "But nothing on you, Sissy."

A woman's voice called through the crowd from behind them. "Alan! Alan, come here."

He handed the baby to Sissy, who held Gene tightly, kissing his face, seeing Elijah in his eyelashes, Elijah whom she loved. She hurried to his side.

THAT NIGHT in their hotel room, Sissy was cheerful.

Her dog Oak had taken Best of Breed. He was the puppy she'd named Acorn, but he'd grown into such a muscular, handsome dog that he'd become Oak. She was happy, too, that the show was over. She liked it when Elijah came with her, but she couldn't stop thinking about Clark's being there, too, and the chance Elijah would see the likeness between her former fiancé and Ezra.

Now they were in bed, the dogs sleeping in crates around them. They had four German shepherds with them and two more at home, plus Belle, Whiteout and Five the cat. Gene still slept with his parents, here as well as at home where they didn't have a room for him yet. They needed to move, which meant selling the house in which they were living and buying another. Elijah wanted to move back to Echo Springs to be near his mother, but it might mean leaving his job at the Humane Society and returning to law enforcement. Sissy knew she would make less money teaching obedience classes in Echo Springs. They also had looked at other communities around the Lake of the Ozarks; the most appealing was Osage Beach. Sissy had suggested opening a pet supply and gift store on the Strip.

Elijah wasn't keen on this. Sissy had two children, taught Obedience classes and had a kennel. He'd noticed, too, that she seemed to constantly want to change her focus in life. She'd stopped writing plays, but had starred in one production at the community theater, then had started teaching dance classes, then had stopped. She was like a person trying on different outfits and tossing each aside as not quite right. And she seemed oblivious to their financial situation. Her excursion into community theater had cost them more than two hundred dollars in babysitting. Elijah hadn't begrudged her that, thought she deserved time to herself, but she sometimes seemed incapable of saying no to herself when it came to new clothes, to something unnecessary for herself or the children.

As Gene lay asleep between them on the bed and Ezra on his own cot, Sissy gazed at Elijah's hand lying near hers on top of the cover. His hands were large and strong-looking, and she saw the wedding ring he never removed and longed for him as she had since she was twelve. Sometimes she thought her desire and need was stronger than his, yet he still touched her with the same attentive, thoroughly engrossed care. She said, "You'll never leave me, will you, Elijah?"

"Not in this life," he said.

Sissy sighed. "I told my mother I'm having nothing more to do with her. My father is always welcome in our home, but she's not."

"Sissy." Elijah sounded distressed.

"I can't stand it anymore. She's never gotten over my marrying you, and she never will."

"Don't blow it up," he said. "It doesn't matter. Just let it be."

"It matters to me!"

"You're not going to change her by doing this."

"How do you know?" Sissy demanded.

Elijah didn't answer at once. "Because that kind of thing never works. Not for change. Not for good."

"I'm not going to let her get away with it," Sissy said, almost to herself, and heard how childish she sounded and didn't care. "You're the most important thing in my life."

"Then do something for me." Elijah touched her cheek. "Don't burn any bridges. It's a bad habit."

June 3, 1978
Echo Springs, Missouri

IT WAS THE LAST THING they'd expected. Alan Atherton had died of a heart attack, and when his will was read, he had left the family's house on the shore of the Lake of the Ozarks to Sissy and Elijah.

Even after his death and the discovery of their inheritance, Elijah and Sissy's decision to move had taken a year and unexpected windfalls, including Elijah's publication of a well-received book. Elijah would continue his work as an investigator from Echo Springs. Sissy was to teach drama part-time at the local high school.

When they sold the house in Kansas City, they'd been able to expand the Athertons' small cabin and create the kennel runs they needed.

Sissy's doubts about the move were that she would be farther from some dog shows (though closer to a few others), and her new location would be less convenient for prospective puppy buyers to visit.

But here there was less chance of seeing Clark Treffinger-Hart—or, more to the point, of Elijah's seeing him.

She could not lose Elijah. She wanted to believe that his knowing the truth would make no difference, but how could it not? Especially after all this time.

She should have told him immediately, the first time they'd made love, that she'd had other lovers.

Yes, they had disagreements, but on most subjects they were of one mind. He was an excellent father, truly the husband of her dreams. He'd even become as interested in the kennel as she was. He made minute observations of the dogs and their interaction with one another. He spent hours writing about them, and Sissy, reading his book before publication, had been surprised by his skill with words. Though she wasn't sure why she should be—he'd always been a good student. Strangely, his way with the dogs reminded her painfully of her father. When she'd told him this, he'd said, "Thank you," and hurried out of the room. She'd seen that it was to hide tears; he missed her father as much as she did.

A motorboat went by towing a skier, and Gene said, "I'd like to go to the beach, Mother." Like Ezra, Gene was very articulate, but he was a strange child. He always spoke almost without inflection. He frustrated Sissy because he seemed unable to grasp basic things about getting along with his brother—or anyone else for that matter. He also seemed to be a bit of a problem for his teacher when he'd started school in Echo Springs that April. His teacher called him "uncooperative" and said he didn't care about the other children's feelings.

Admittedly he had many habits Sissy thought strange. For instance, what he did on the "beach," at the lake's edge, was find pebbles of nearly identical size and arrange them on the wall. He refused to go in the water, screaming and shrieking if anyone attempted to take him in. Elijah had at first insisted, even briefly swimming away from Gene, returning only when it was clear that Gene would not fend for himself and seemed likely to drown. Finally he and Sissy had both realized it was hopeless.

Gene was a bit clumsy anyhow, and didn't care to go for walks or play running games or throw balls.

She'd said once to Elijah, "You need to deal with Gene more the way you do with the dogs."

Ever since, Elijah's attitude toward his younger son had changed dramatically. He did not try to make Gene do things he didn't want to do. He didn't try to break him of strange habits. He mutely observed the way Gene simply issued matter-of-fact commands to the people around him. *Mother, I'd like to go to the beach now.* When confronted by Gene's utter disinterest in being cuddled or held or even kissed good-night, Elijah simply shrugged.

Sissy found nearly all of these habits more than aggravating, but she, too, had learned that Gene could not be won to other viewpoints by persuasion, by begging, by tears, by anything. There had been incidents at school, too, particularly of his running away. Well, he was new to the school environment.

"Yes. You and Ezra, get your life jackets," she told Gene. She and Elijah agreed completely about rules for the children near the water. They were not to go on the dock alone, were not to swim unaccompanied by an adult (an unnecessary mandate in Gene's case) and wore life vests when they played by the water. Sissy sometimes let Ezra remove his when she was with him, to improve his swimming.

The phone rang, and Sissy stood and left the sunshine to answer it.

"Hi." Kennedy.

The unexpected legacy left to Sissy and Elijah had created no bitterness between the sisters, perhaps because Alan Atherton had left his violin to Kennedy, which was what she'd most wanted.

"Hey, there," Sissy answered, trying to inject some enthusiasm into her voice.

"Mother just left."

"I'm sorry." Her mother had cut off all contact with Sissy after the reading of her husband's will, except to briefly challenge the will in court. There was no one who didn't interpret his gift to Sissy and Elijah as condemnation of Heloise Atherton's attitude toward them.

"She wants Ellen started in ballet. My God, she's two-and-a-half, and it's all Mom can talk about."

Sissy smiled to herself. "When are you coming down to stay with us?"

"It will be a little while. Gerry has so many patients right now, most of them determined to have their babies in the dead of night, usually when I could really use him at home."

The conversation was brief, and afterward, Sissy took the boys swimming. When they were back inside and Gene napping and Ezra busy in his room with Lego, Sissy went out to clean the kennels and the fenced lawn. Elijah would be home soon.

As soon as she had the thought, his car drove down the steep gravel drive, and she abandoned her task and went to meet him.

His smile was exclusively for her, full of the radiant love he felt for her. He clasped her in his arms as they stood on the gravel drive, kissed her hair, said, "You are so beautiful, Sissy."

She kissed him back, said, "How was work?" And, "I think we need some new floatation in the dock. Shall we work on that this weekend?" They frequently worked together on the property, and this gave Elijah, in particular, a serenity he associated with the perfect meshing of their lives into one life.

As he started to respond, a child's wail sounded from the dogs' yard.

It was not an ordinary cry, the kind that she would walk towards calmly. It was a shrieking howl. Sissy, still close to Elijah, broke free and ran around the corner of the house to find Ezra on the grass, holding his arm, sobbing. He looked strange, his color grayish, and she saw in horror the puncture marks.

"Sissy, stay calm," said Elijah. To Ezra, "Where's the snake?"

Ezra pointed toward the lawn, and Sissy said, "Who cares about the snake? We have to go to the—"

Elijah ignored her. He picked up a head-sized rock, strode across the lawn and dropped it. "Nothing poisonous. You'll be okay, buddy," he told Ezra. "Still, I'll run him over to the hospital. Best to make sure there's no bacterial infection."

Nothing poisonous.

Sissy said, "No, I'll get Gene. You get in the car."

Sissy scooped Gene out of bed, and he blinked

open and immediately squirmed to be put down. "Hurry with me. We have to go in the car."

"No," Gene said.

"Yes," she said, unwilling to yield on this occasion.

Gene sat down on the floor right where he was. She picked him up, and he began to scream.

He screamed in the car on the way to the hospital, and curled himself in a ball sobbing inconsolably.

On the way to the hospital, Ezra's arm swelled and his color grew worse. He cried out in pain. Sissy told Elijah, "Get there faster! And, Gene, *stop it!*"

Gene, of course, ignored her completely.

"Just relax," Elijah said.

But he was breaking the speed limit and then some.

At the hospital, he grabbed Ezra and the dead snake in the bag and ran inside. Sissy dashed around to get Gene out, but he wouldn't leave the car, so she locked him in with the windows partway down. She ran into the hospital to see Elijah shoving the paper bag at the emergency room doctor, who looked inside, nodded, and shot orders at a nurse.

Sissy grabbed the bag and looked in it. A young snake, its copper-colored head smashed. "You knew," she said. He'd deliberately subdued her fear—and Ezra's.

"You're supposed to keep snakebite victims calm," he said.

ELIJAH STOOD outside Ezra's hospital room, gazing stupidly at the chart hanging beside the door.

Sissy would not leave Ezra's side, which required their hiring frequent babysitters to stay with Gene, who refused to go to the hospital and screamed the entire time if he was forced to do so. Elijah couldn't think about that now, only about Ezra.

He's going to live. He's going to live. Yet Elijah kept praying, and he gazed sightlessly at the chart.

Our Father, who art in Heaven…

NAME: Ezra James Workman. BIRTHDATE: 3/11/1970

Hallowed be Thy name…

His eyes read the orders. Ezra had received blood. AB+.

Thy kingdom come, Thy will be done…

Elijah blinked. Sissy's was… He'd thought it was A+. Obviously he must be wrong. It must be AB+. No… That wouldn't make the difference. He was O+. He remembered high school biology, pricking his own finger, identifying his own blood type under a magnifying glass. And he remembered that his offspring, because he was O+, would never have AB type blood.

Could the chart be wrong?

He'd seen Ezra receiving blood, and Ezra had suffered no ill effects.

Elijah stared at the chart, wondering if he was reading the nurse's writing incorrectly. No. Very clear. AB+.

This can't be true.

Maybe *his* blood type… After all, he was the one who'd typed it in biology, and he'd never received a blood transfusion.

But you've given blood, Elijah.

It couldn't be right, couldn't be right that Ezra's blood type was AB+. Because if it was true…

The empty blood bag might still be in the trash can in the room.

And Elijah could walk into the room and see.

But he didn't need to.

Because he suddenly knew that he was not Ezra Workman's biological father.

And he had a very good idea who was.

CHAPTER EIGHT

I asked, "Why did you fight her when you knew she'd just get hurt?"
He said, "I didn't think about her hurting. I just thought about the money, and how bad *I* was. You know. Ego."
—*On the Side of the Dogs,* Elijah Workman, 2008

The same afternoon, 1978

WHEN ELIJAH STARTED his car outside the hospital, the radio came on, a top-forty DJ taunting him with golden oldies. The Everly Brothers and the song he'd once thought the most beautiful love song in the world, beautiful because she loved it.

He started to switch it off but stopped himself. Then came the pain behind his eyes, and he did wrench at the knob, turning off the music as he put his head in his arms on the steering wheel. *God…* She'd lied.

For years.

He turned the radio back on, changed the station to the public radio station and tried to listen to the news while he drove home.

The babysitter met him in the driveway, looking worried. At first Elijah thought she wanted to know about Ezra, but that wasn't it.

"I'm sorry. I don't know what to do with him. He's in the kennel."

Gene.

Fourteen-year-old Candy was the daughter of one of Kennedy's high school friends. She was a responsible brunette with glasses, who always came equipped with homework, but she made sure she played with the boys—well, with Ezra. Gene wouldn't have much to do with her.

Elijah approached the kennel run in question, occupied by Martha and two of her offspring, both less than six months old. He couldn't see Gene, which made him suppose the boy had actually gone into the dogs' shelter. "What happened?" he asked Candy.

"He wanted to go to the beach, and I just checked his life vest to see if it was tight enough, and he ran away. Then he found a scorpion and didn't want to go to the beach anymore. I told him he couldn't play with the scorpion, and I took it away from him, and he went into the kennels. The dog growled at me and wouldn't let me in."

Elijah opened the kennel door, and Martha trotted happily toward him.

Elijah petted her once and walked down to the doghouse at the end. One of the puppies poked his head out, then emerged to greet Elijah.

Gene was curled up in the doghouse with his favorite blanket and a flashlight, reading a children's book about spiders that he had read many times before and knew by heart. He could also tell Elijah how many letters were in the entire book, including and excluding title and copyright pages.

Elijah said, "Hello."

Gene turned off his flashlight, picked up his book and blanket, and came out of the doghouse. Without saying a word, he walked out of the kennel, shutting the door behind him, and went back to the house.

June 5, 1978

EZRA CAME HOME from the hospital Sunday afternoon. Elijah and Sissy had been coming and going from the hospital, had hardly slept in the same bed since Ezra's snakebite. Elijah took over much of the kennel work because Sissy hated to leave Ezra's side, but on Sunday afternoon she joined him as she cleaned up the yard.

Julia approached Sissy repeatedly with her ball, wanting it thrown. Watching Sissy with the beautiful bitch, Elijah's chest grew tight. He had not told Sissy of his discovery at the hospital. Instead, he brooded over the knowledge, asking himself questions to which he might never know the answers. Did Sissy know that Ezra was not Elijah's biological son? Was Ezra Clark's son— or, appallingly, someone else's yet? Elijah thought he must be Clark's. If he confronted Sissy now, would she be truthful with him?

For the time being, he said nothing, not knowing what to say. If Ezra was Clark's son, shouldn't Clark have the right to know him? It was unreasonable to feel as though Sissy had been unfaithful to him, and Elijah didn't feel that. But dishonest?

She had to know that Ezra wasn't his son.

He supposed it was something stubborn in him that resisted telling her. Because he was angry. *Why* hadn't she told him? It seemed devious, and he couldn't see the reason behind the lie. Had she been afraid he'd leave her? Or wouldn't love Ezra?

He'd believed she was a virgin. Or had he? He'd never asked. Was that because he hadn't wanted to know about any other relationships she'd had? *Maybe so, Elijah.* Maybe so.

Sissy said, "I want to go to the German Shepherd Nationals this year, Elijah."

He shrugged. "We'll have to save for that." Before they'd begun to do it together, he'd had no idea how expensive showing dogs could be.

"Well, it's a business expense," Sissy said. "We have to make a place for it, and that's that."

Elijah just nodded.

Sissy watched him covertly. She'd become an expert on Elijah over the years of her marriage. When angry or bothered about something, he became aloof. And ever since Ezra's snakebite, he'd been remote as the arctic. He hadn't even turned to her to make love in the few hours they'd found each other together in bed. "Are you all right, Elijah?"

Elijah blinked, seeming to come out of a trance. "Yes," he said, unsure why he avoided the real issue, just knowing he couldn't voice the truth, couldn't speak it. "Sure."

That evening, when the children were asleep, the air cool in the house because of the air conditioner's intermittent hum, they lay in bed together. Dogs in crates around the edges of the bedroom, and Whiteout, Teddy and Belle finding their own spots.

Elijah didn't turn to her, so Sissy reached for him, touched his shoulder, sensed the strong, hot beat of his heart.

Then he rolled toward her, and she saw the whites of his eyes in the dark. She touched his face, kissed him, and he kissed her back, his mouth opening slowly, licking her lips, then the inside of her mouth. He seemed almost tentative, as though this was the first time they'd ever done this. But he soon embraced her, drew her closer.

Sissy felt a desperation to be one with him and was glad for his hands caressing her in their worshipful way, stirring a vibration of light through her. She cried out softly, pulling him closer.

Afterward, when they separated, he held her gently. Her cheek lay against his heart, her favorite pose with him. He stroked her hair, and she believed for the moment that they were close. His remoteness was just a mood and would pass as it always did.

June 8, 1979

KENNEDY WORKMAN ARRIVED in the world with the caul over her head at 3:00 p.m. after Sissy's longest and worst labor—twenty-nine hours. She had accepted nothing for pain, however. Now, two days after the birth, she and Kennedy were home.

Something had happened to Sissy in the past year. At first, Elijah sensed a despair in her, the reasons for which he hadn't been able to pinpoint. Then she seemed to fold in on herself, living her life as though it didn't include Elijah, Ezra or Gene. Especially Gene. According to his new teacher's mixed reports, he seemed very bright, especially at math, memorizing flash cards after one look, but he was "uncooperative" and "careless of the feelings of others." Sissy told Elijah, "You deal with it. You're the behavior expert."

Because he'd published a book on canine behavior.

One day she'd announced, "I'm writing another play. They're going to put it on at Sarah Lawrence."

The play had turned out to be about a couple gradually growing apart while the wife came to care more for her dogs than for her family because her husband did not care for her.

Elijah had gotten the picture. He'd said, "Sissy, I *do* love you. God, you're my wife."

She had said, "You think people love each other just because they're married? Look at my parents."

One of whom was now dead and who had left property to someone other than his wife.

But Elijah remembered when the Athertons had seemed to love each other. Had they grown apart because of their different feelings about his marrying Sissy? Well, that wasn't his responsibility.

Yet he'd never liked Sissy's estrangement from her mother.

Two days after Kennedy's birth, Elijah sat in the shade on the deck, holding his newborn daughter while Sissy slept. He had the week off from work so as to spend time with his family.

He and Sissy had both changed since they were married, and lately he'd begun to wonder if Sissy still loved him. Several times in the past months, she'd remarked, "You're very traditional," and he'd begun to see that she viewed this as a limitation.

He sometimes suspected that she actively disliked Gene. Maybe because he hated being cuddled, hugged or kissed, maybe because his teacher had started talking about "child psychologists."

Ezra came out and sat beside Elijah. Elijah had been surprised to find his feelings for Ezra were completely unchanged since he'd learned the boy wasn't his biological child. He was too used to thinking of Ezra as his son, to feeling pride in him, to having a relationship with him. Now Ezra said, "Dad, could we have an exterminator?"

Elijah knew why. The scorpions. For some reason, there were more of them than usual this year, and he'd found two in the house, one blending in perfectly with the light-colored carpet. They weren't dangerous unless someone was allergic to them, but their sting would be very painful. Ezra, who'd been bitten by a copperhead, had developed a bit of a phobia about them.

Elijah considered the question. "They're

coming in from outside, Ezra. Even if we tented the house and fumigated, more would come in. We have to just keep looking out for them, and eventually they will go away."

Ezra peered down at Kennedy's small face. "Can I hold her?"

"Sure." Elijah moved to the outdoor loveseat, and Ezra sat beside him. Elijah positioned the infant in Ezra's lap and watched his son touch the baby's small hand. It was ironic, Elijah sometimes thought, how much he loved this child, occasionally more than Gene, who was his own blood. But there was something special about Ezra, a curiosity that reminded Elijah of Alan Atherton—and, strangely, of himself.

Ezra said, "Michael told me a water skier fell down in a school of water moccasins that were mating. He got bitten all over and died."

Michael was Ezra's best friend from school. His parents were people Sissy had always known from her country club connections.

This story was familiar to Elijah. He'd never heard it substantiated. "The odds of that happening are slim. It's probably more likely you'll be struck by lightning, and that's not very likely."

Ezra said, "Were you and Mother trying for a girl?"

This was bizarre. "What gave you that idea?"

"Michael's mom said you probably were."

"Well, we weren't," Elijah said. "But I'm very happy with Kennedy. It will be fun to have a girl around."

"If you say so," Ezra replied without enthusiasm. But he smiled at Kennedy. "She's very cute, though."

Elijah stared down at Kennedy's face and wondered what she would be like. Like Sissy as an adolescent? Elijah felt his hair stand up at the thought. An indefinite sixth sense warned him of more changes to come in the world around him, changes he'd find hard to understand.

Gene came outside. Like Ezra, he had been with a babysitter during the birth. Sissy had wanted them to see their sibling born. Elijah had thought it inappropriate. She'd said he was old-fashioned. But it was impossible anyhow, in Gene's case, once Gene had learned the baby would be born at the hospital.

Now Gene looked at Kennedy dispassionately. He was carrying one of his favorite things, the telephone book. He sat by himself on a chair and began to read.

Unhappily, Elijah pondered the concerns of Gene's teacher. He thought he knew what was wrong, knew because he'd gone to the library to try to find more information, then had talked to a friend whose child was extremely gifted.

But Gene wasn't just gifted. *Did he get it from me?* Elijah wondered. One of his brothers had been a bit like Gene; now he was a car mechanic living in California. No marriage, no girlfriend, not brilliant at getting along with others. But it wasn't supposed to be genetic, was it?

Hoping for a different sort of answer than what he expected, he asked, "Would you like to hold your sister, Gene?"

Gene never looked up from the phone book. "No."

HOURS LATER, Sissy lay in the bedroom with Kennedy at her breast. Already there was confusion over which Kennedy they were talking about when they spoke of the baby or of Sissy's sister. So Kennedy was becoming Eddy, which Sissy rather liked.

Sissy heard Elijah in the next room cooking dinner and telling Ezra to let his mother sleep. He was a good husband, and he loved her. He'd changed his job and returned to Echo Springs because of her wishes. He preferred being in the field as an investigator to working as director of the local Humane Society, but he had accepted the latter position. What was more, he was constantly drawing fire because he, with Sissy, bred dogs.

The phone rang, and Sissy wondered if it

would be Kennedy, calling to tell her their mother's reaction to the birth. Sissy had refused to let Elijah call Heloise after Eddy's birth. After all, her mother had shown no interest in her pregnancy. It was as though Heloise had only one daughter.

Sissy reached for the phone, watching Eddy's tiny face. The newborn squinted, and Sissy feared she'd wake up, but she didn't.

"Hello?"

"Is Sissy there?" A man.

"This is Sissy."

Elijah opened the bedroom door and looked in. Sissy smiled to let him know everything was okay.

He crossed the room and kissed her smooth forehead, stroking her hair back from her face.

"Sissy, it's Clark."

Sissy's heart stopped. These had been glowing days. She had a new daughter, and she was in love with her beautiful, magical child, the girl born with a caul over her head. Yet here was an intruder.

"Yes."

Elijah stood looking down at her, his expression inquisitive.

"Berkeley's birthday is coming up, and she wants a shepherd. To show. We looked at your mom's dogs, but Berkeley really likes your bitch who took Winner's Bitch two weeks ago."

"Martha," Sissy said. "I just bred her to Samson, you know that black-and-tan male of Gerard's that's out of Weather Station. That may be a little late for you if there's a birthday involved…" Sissy almost hoped he would reject that possibility of buying one of her puppies. The thought of two experienced handlers like Clark and Berkeley showing one of her puppies weighed against fear of Elijah looking at Clark, seeing a resemblance between her ex and Ezra. But that worry was really just silly.

"Oh, you know, Sissy," Clark said warmly. "She wants her pick, and she'd prefer to wait and get the puppy she really wants. I don't know Samson, but I'll see if Berkeley does."

"I have photos of him and Martha if you'd like me to put them in the mail to you."

"That would be great."

Sissy reached for a pen and pad on the bedside table. Elijah said, "Want me to get the information?"

Sissy shook her head.

A moment later, when she'd hung up, she said, "That was Clark. He and his wife are interested in one of our puppies."

Elijah did not point out that they had no puppies on the ground. He'd heard enough to gather the rest of the conversation.

He looked at Kennedy sleeping beside Sissy. He should not upset the new mother. This stopped him from saying, "Ever planning to tell him Ezra is his son?"

The devil was, Ezra looked like Clark. Surely Clark might spot the resemblance. Elijah remembered the one dog show where he'd seen Clark examining the children with interest. Had Clark seen a resemblance then?

Don't say it, he cautioned himself. *Not now.* There would be time later. Martha's puppies, if the breeding had been successful, wouldn't be born for weeks. Plenty of time for him to query the wisdom of bringing Clark around their house and their family.

Or, alternately, to suggest that it was only fair to tell him that Ezra was his natural son.

Elijah supposed that was part of what bothered him about Sissy's apparent take on the situation. She seemed undisturbed by Ezra's never knowing his biological father—and by Clark's never knowing his son.

I can't bring it up now, he counseled himself again, nearly exploding with the need to do so.

Instead, he said, "Can I get you something?" He saw her big empty juice bottle, which she used for a water glass when she was nursing, and he picked it up. "More water, anyway."

July 3, 1979

ELIJAH HAD SPENT the last year treating Sissy as though nothing was different between them. In fact, nothing was. Ezra had always been Clark Treffinger-Hart's biological son. Now Elijah knew about it; that was the only change.

His tradition had been to give Sissy a dog-related present every anniversary, usually something silly that concealed something romantic. Last year, devastated by what he'd discovered after Ezra's snakebite, he'd had trouble summoning the energy and had settled on some fourteen-karat gold earrings shaped like German shepherds.

This year had been even harder. He still loved Sissy, but their relationship now felt unreal to him. She was lying to him about Ezra; he was lying to her about knowing about Ezra.

Anyhow, why give someone a dog gift when they had the real thing, these incredibly beautiful animals that surpassed humans in their ability to love and, most of all, to forgive. People said animals had no free will, but Elijah remembered warning Bonnie, a sable female who liked to knock over puppies, that if she did it again she'd have a time-out. As one of the puppies had walked past her, Bonnie had looked at the puppy, then at Elijah. Quite deliberately, she'd knocked the puppy over. Then, before he could more than take one step toward her, she'd headed straight into her crate for time-out. No free will? Right.

This year, for their anniversary, he'd asked a local artist whom Sissy admired to paint Teddy's portrait. Teddy was thirteen, with gray on his muzzle, and Sissy loved him profoundly. Elijah, on the pretense of taking the dog to the park to "work on obedience" and "observe him," had brought Teddy to sit for the painter. Now, as dinnertime approached and he waited for Sissy to return from a tennis match with Allie Morgan, her childhood friend whose family's cabin was two houses down, it occurred to him that he'd gone to the trouble with Teddy to prove to himself that he loved Sissy exactly as he always had.

And he recognized, too, that it wasn't true at all.

But when she came in, when she unwrapped the present that had taken such time and money and trouble and turned to him with shining eyes, he saw that she saw nothing different in him, nothing different between them. So he supposed it had been worth it for that.

September 10, 1979

ELIJAH STOOD in a farmyard less than a quarter mile from the gas station where he had first met Lucky, decades before. It was Vincent Cory's farmyard. Police and Humane Society workers hurried about, working, talking. Photographers from two newspapers and a television camera crew had arrived. Elijah wore a suit jacket, his tie loose, and a pair of Wellies he kept in the trunk of his car for such occasions. He could not bring the filth of this place back to his home, his kennels, especially not to Martha's new litter. He crouched beside the body of a pit bull bitch, worn out by multiple breedings, emaciated, now fed upon by insects, then got up and walked away, heading for one of the outbuildings where Vince Cory had been raising toy breeds.

Here, the brood bitches had had the worst time. Toys didn't birth easily at the best of times. Elijah was numb, numb to what he saw around him. He'd become numb from overexposure to such things. Then there was the fact that Eddy awoke and cried from 1:00 a.m. till 5:00 a.m. every night. Sissy nursed her, and then Elijah walked with her, singing to her, talking to her, telling her he wished he could understand what she needed to stop crying.

And now, within, oh, ten minutes, he could look forward to some member of the press asking if didn't he breed dogs in his backyard? How could he justify doing that while there were so many unwanted dogs in the world?

And he would give the same answers again.

He would say that he and Sissy were not "backyard breeders," that their dogs' hips and elbows, temperament and more, were thoroughly tested before they were bred. Furthermore, his dogs were also pets, members of the family. They slept inside with their masters. Genesis German shepherd dogs had been featured in *The German Shepherd Quarterly,* and so on.

But weren't there enough dogs in the world already? the reporters would persist.

Sometimes, Elijah wanted to shout that no, there weren't, there were just too many rotten people. He'd juggled his career and the kennels for, well, really just for six years or so, and it had become more of an issue as time wore on. None of these people would have trouble with any of the neglected or abused animals he'd rescued over the years becoming his pet, but start raising dogs who will never be abused and people screamed, "Hypocrite!"

Ten minutes later, he answered those same questions. "Actually, we do spay and neuter our animals that we don't want to breed. Now, are there more questions about what we've discovered here?"

"Mr. Workman, do you think there are more puppy mills in our area?"

"We hope not. The Humane Society is remaining vigilant in investigating suspected puppy mills and making sure they're closed down and the people responsible brought to justice. We invite the public to call us if they note any suspicious activity that might suggest the existence of a puppy mill."

"Mr. Workman," asked the television journalist. "Is it true the puppy mill owner in this case was also involved in illegal dogfights?"

"We're looking into that. And *all* staged dogfights are illegal." He thought of his uncle Silas, who had died two years before. Elijah had found homes for Silas's dogs, fostering them at his own place rather than letting them be put down.

When Elijah returned to his car, he changed shoes and threw the Wellingtons in the trunk again, moving Sissy's tennis racket. She had recently begun playing tennis at the country club. She was not a member; Elijah could not afford it.

Elijah noticed that the people she was seeing the most were those she'd been friends with when they were in high school, and their social network revolved around the country club. He thought of that as he returned home that evening and found Sissy sitting on the deck with Eddy and their neighbor Allie Morgan.

Walking out onto the deck, Elijah found Sissy laughing hard at something Allie had said.

He sat down with them, and Ezra came out of the house and climbed into his lap. Sissy said to Allie, "And what are they going to do about that?" continuing a conversation about Allie's brother, Jay, and his wife.

"Well, they're going to take him to a specialist. It's the only way to find out what's wrong."

Elijah said, "What's this?"

"My brother's son. He has—I guess you'd call them behavioral problems. He doesn't like to be around people. He gets very upset when things don't go his way."

That sounded a bit familiar to Elijah. "Does he do all right in school?"

Allie rolled her eyes. "How could he? I mean, grade school is largely about learning to get along with others, and he simply can't deal with that."

Elijah gave Sissy a meaningful look. He had a feeling though, that Gene's problems—or the decision about whether *he* should see a specialist—might be taken out of their hands by the school.

Sissy determinedly avoided his gaze. She insisted Gene was just "a difficult child." That was putting things mildly, though she was sometimes obviously hurt by Gene's lack of affection.

Sissy changed the subject, asking him, "How was work?"

Elijah made a slight face. "Puppy mill bust."

"You showered—"

"At work," Elijah finished, not appreciating her tone. He knew better than she the diseases rampant at puppy mills, and that the lives of Martha's puppies depended upon not becoming infected.

"Where was it?" Sissy asked in a slightly more conciliatory tone.

"Vince Cory's, believe it or not."

"I believe it," she answered. "I bet he's been matching dogs, too." She also remembered that Elijah's first dog, Lucky, had been a victim of Vince Cory's cruelty.

"If so, the details will probably come out," Elijah admitted, taking off his tie, which Ezra then proceeded to try to put on. Ezra, who Sissy undoubtedly still believed she was passing off as Elijah's son. That lie was so destructive he couldn't contemplate it. What he cared about these days was Gene. What to do about Gene.

He counted Sissy, Eddy, Ezra, two German shepherds and Belle lounging on the deck. Whiteout had passed away that summer, and Elijah still missed him. Belle sniffed him out and lay at his feet. "Where's Gene?" he asked Sissy.

"His room," she said, "probably reading."

As though Gene was just your average slightly bookish kid.

Which he was not.

SISSY LAY ON THE BED nursing Eddy when Elijah came in and lay beside her in his sweatpants and a Humane Society T-shirt, still looking lean and hard. But also, she saw him as her deeply traditional husband, and sometimes she found that side of him limiting.

Sissy gazed into his brown eyes. *I'm still so in love with you,* she thought. And he was a good husband. But so damned aloof, as though he'd put up a wall between them. She'd never come up with a good reason for his distance from her. She'd wondered if it was just his grief over her father's death, but the timing wasn't quite right.

As Eddy dropped off to sleep, Sissy moved the infant onto her stomach and readjusted her nursing bra. "Elijah, can you tell me what's wrong?"

"I'm thinking about Gene. He needs to see someone."

"He's not that strange!" Sissy immediately exclaimed. "He just—I don't know. He's different. He's smart."

Yes. An I.Q. test at school had put him at 155. But his teachers still had questions about him.

And Elijah thought of his son, pictured his strange mechanical gait, heard his flat voice, a voice without inflection. "I've wondered if it could be a kind of autism."

Sissy stared at him. "Autistic people don't talk, Elijah. Not like Gene."

"Some of them do. Some have good language skills. Sissy, he knows how many numbers are in the phone book. Not just how many phone numbers—the total number of digits. And think about his thing with arachnids."

Sissy shuddered slightly. She shared Ezra's distaste for scorpions, but Gene seemed to like spiders and, especially, scorpions to the exclusion of everything else, reading way beyond his grade level, memorizing their Latin names. He captured both spiders and scorpions, kept them in jars in his room, captured insects for them. He talked about them incessantly. Nonetheless… "What about it? He's bright. And he likes dogs, too."

"No," Elijah said. "He trusts dogs." The kennel had become Gene's favorite hiding place when he was upset. Besides Martha, his favorite of the dogs was Oak, who seemed to regard him as a son or nephew, a puppy. But Elijah had noticed that, though Gene felt safe with the dogs, his interest was not of the passionate kind he felt for scorpions. "And, Sissy, he doesn't have normal reactions to other people's feelings. When you get mad at him, sometimes he doesn't even notice."

Sissy blinked. "What does all this mean?"

"It means—I don't know. I don't know what they can do, but he's going to need special help. We should deal with this sooner rather than later."

"Elijah, I don't think he's handicapped, and I don't want you taking him to someone who's going to say he is!"

"I don't think anyone's going to say that. But we need to take him to the doctors and find out just what he needs."

"Fine," Sissy said.

Elijah reached toward her, touched her hair, tried not to think of the differences between Ezra and Gene, about the fact that Gene was of his blood and Ezra was not.

But Sissy grabbed him, holding him. She whispered, "God, why are you so damned aloof sometimes? Sometimes you remind me of him."

Of Gene.

Elijah started to back away, but Sissy clung to the muscles beneath his neck, feeling his strong shoulders, his back. She put her hands beneath his T-shirt. "I think we need to use birth control, don't you?"

He kissed her, wondering if he could make love with her. Had that remark had anything to do with Gene? No, of course not. Eddy was his child, too, and she was fine. Though Gene, at Eddy's age, had seemed like any other baby.

The telephone's ringing broke into his thought and saved him from uncertainty and pretense.

"THEY'RE COMING TOMORROW to see the puppies."

Elijah nodded. "Ah."

Sissy did not quite meet his eyes. "I hope they take Pink Girl."

Their system for distinguishing one puppy from another involved using different colored ribbons as collars. Pink Girl was a pretty black-and-tan bitch, one of the two best in the litter.

"You're sure you want to let her go?" Elijah thought of the lines Genesis was developing, the dogs they wanted to produce. But he also thought of Ezra, of Clark, of Sissy's deception.

"Well, they'll show her, and they're both good handlers. Anyhow, we have so many bitches right now, we'll let them choose."

Elijah gazed at her for a moment. "You're not worried about Clark discovering that Ezra is his son."

Sissy's stomach sucked in as though she'd been kicked. For a moment she couldn't quite breathe. *He knows.* Her mouth dropped as she wondered if she should deny it.

"I *assume* he's Clark's," Elijah said. "Unless there was someone else?"

Sissy thought she might throw up. His look

wasn't cold, but she wondered if *this* was what lay behind his aloofness. And knew that it must be. "How…long have you known?" she managed to say.

"Since the copperhead bite. I saw his blood type on his chart."

Sissy tried to speak, then simply tried to swallow. "Why didn't you say?"

He shrugged. "Maybe I thought you might."

It wasn't true, Sissy knew. He must have known that, having kept the secret since Ezra's birth, she'd intended to keep it always. "Maybe you should be sincere," she said.

"Me?" He lifted his eyebrows.

She sagged. She'd been sitting up against the pillows. She seemed to shrink into herself. "Elijah, I had sex with him just once. I can't even call it making love," she whispered. "I did it to convince myself to go through with the wedding, but it had the opposite effect. It was awful. But it was part of why I left him at the altar. I *knew* I didn't love him."

Elijah made himself sit near her on the bed. "What I don't understand," he said, "is why you never told me." Some of the feelings he'd been keeping to himself for more than a year poured out. "You were never going to tell me? You were never going to tell Ezra? And what about Clark?"

"He has nothing to do with this," Sissy said.

Elijah refrained from choking dramatically.

"Ezra is *our* son," she said. "Yours and mine."

Elijah told her, "I don't think that's your decision to make."

"Well, it's certainly not *yours*," she exclaimed. "I'm his mother. I gave birth to him."

Elijah gazed at her long straight hair, the well-defined bones of her face, her perfect white teeth, and wondered if she'd always been so arrogant. On some level, *yes,* he decided. "And I suppose you think I have that little to do with Gene and Eddy, too?"

She drew a deliberate breath. "All right, I don't mean that about Ezra. He's your son, and of course we have to make decisions about him together. I just don't see any point in taking this further. He doesn't need to know, and Clark doesn't need to know, either."

Elijah seemed to squint at her, as though trying to make out something far away. "What are you afraid of?"

"I'm not *afraid.* I just think this is better for everyone."

"Why?" he asked flatly.

"Don't you think we have enough trouble?"

Elijah said, "I don't like deception."

"Well, you've sure been enjoying it since Ezra's snakebite," she snapped.

"I haven't been *enjoying* it. I've been wondering why in hell you never told me the truth. Did you think I'd leave you or something?"

Sissy looked at him, her violet eyes oddly challenging. "Actually, yes. That's what I thought. Or, more precisely, I thought you'd want to leave, but would be a martyr and stay."

Elijah tried to play it through his mind. When Sissy had first become pregnant, say she'd said, *Elijah, there's a chance this is Clark's baby.* It would have made no difference to him!

But the assertion rang through him like a lie. He didn't really believe it. The truth was that he couldn't imagine how he would have felt. He'd been in love with Sissy. He would have been disappointed that the child wasn't his.

Was he in love with Sissy now?

Not that it mattered. He'd married her, and being married meant less about being in love than about commitment, keeping a sacred promise, a different and deeper kind of love.

And this beautiful woman was his lifetime partner. She was strong-willed, could be bossy, but he didn't mind those traits. They were part of her spirit. He just couldn't quite fathom someone keeping the secret she'd kept for so long. He thought of her barbs about his supposedly being "traditional." But she was the one who believed their family perfection would be somehow marred by admitting their unconventionality, by allowing Ezra to deal with his real situation, by allowing him the chance to know his natural father.

By admitting there might be something "wrong" with Gene.

"What makes you think Clark would want anything to do with him?" Sissy hissed, keeping her voice down.

Elijah took a moment to put himself in Clark's shoes.

"If it were me," he said, "I'd want to know. And I'd sure as hell want something to do with him."

"That's because you already know him and love him," Sissy said in a patient tone that made Elijah grit his teeth.

He replied, "That's quite an assumption on your part, Sissy."

"That you know and love your son?"

"No. That…" He didn't want to repeat their whole conversation. "If I were Clark," he said, "I would want to know. And I would want to know Ezra, want him to know me."

"And you blithely think that's a good idea for our son. You think Clark will be a good role model for him?"

Elijah found this argument disingenuous. He said, "Is there some reason you think he *wouldn't* be? Do you know something I don't? Some instance of double handling?" A term for a type of illegal maneuvering in the ring.

"Ha ha. Very funny."

"Or is it the terriers?" he couldn't keep himself from asking.

"Not funny."

Elijah waited to see if she would reveal something damning about Clark.

She didn't.

He made himself say, "I'm not going to leave you. I haven't considered it."

"You're just going to be aloof from me for the rest of our lives," Sissy said. "That's worse."

Aloof. Elijah considered this and remembered how she'd said he was like Gene that way. Elijah hoped that wasn't true. He supposed that being aloof was his way of protecting himself. And he'd seen Sissy do the same thing. He said softly, "You really think it's worse?"

"Yes," she snapped. "I do."

He could think of nothing more to say but to repeat, "I'm not thinking of leaving you."

CHAPTER NINE

Dogs are pack animals. Depriving them of your company and affection is an excellent way to show your displeasure at their behavior.

—*Teach Yourself, Teach Your Dog,* Elijah
Workman, 1973

September 11, 1979

DAMN ELIJAH. He had refused to be present when Clark and Berkeley came to see the puppies. *Unless you plan to tell him the truth and tell him soon.*

Sissy had told him it was blackmail, nothing less, and she added, "Fine. Go to the Strip."

Instead, he'd taken Gene and Ezra to the library and to play miniature golf. Well, Ezra would play miniature golf, Gene would follow them around reading about scorpions or possibly catching insects to feed to his arachnid menagerie.

Elijah had wanted to leave Ezra behind and just take Gene to the library. Sissy knew this wasn't a sign of favoritism, but a way to force her to be in the same room with Clark and Ezra, but Ezra had wanted to play miniature golf, so he went with Elijah.

Sissy greeted Clark and Berkeley at the door, offered them something to drink. Oak was walking beside her, being a gentleman, along with one of the puppies, Dark Blue Boy, a black-and-tan who was a talker and a favorite of Elijah's, to Sissy's annoyance, for he would never be a show dog and they couldn't afford to keep more dogs of pet quality than they possessed.

Belle curled up in her favorite spot under the kitchen table, and Sissy saw Clark eye her askance.

"Elijah rescued her from a research lab," Sissy said.

"Oh, poor thing. Or lucky thing, I should say," put in Berkeley.

Berkeley had short, straight blond hair, which she wore in a Dorothy Hamill cut; while a bit outdated, the style suited her perfectly. She was taller than Sissy—almost six feet—and put her hand out for Oak to sniff.

Sissy poured each of them ice water, then they went out to the lawn, and she let the other puppies out of the kennel.

Berkeley immediately sat on the grass to see which puppies came to her. Sissy picked up Pink Girl, who was carrying a stuffed toy, and brought her over. "This is the one I thought you might really want," she said. "Elijah thinks we should keep her, and it's tempting, but I'll be just as happy if she goes to a good show home."

The runt of the litter, whom she and Elijah had taken to calling Little Girl, crawled into Berkeley's lap. Little Girl had a beautiful face. Berkeley said, "They're all precious."

Sissy excused herself to go inside and check on Eddy, who was napping. Still asleep. Sissy knew she'd wake soon, and her breasts felt full to bursting. She hoped she wouldn't start leaking through her blouse, and she pulled on a cardigan just in case.

She returned to the yard to find Clark crouched beside Pink Girl. "This is a very nice puppy," he said.

Berkeley was playing with Dark Blue Boy.

"The other one," Sissy said, "that I thought might interest you is Red Boy." Red Boy was sable, solidly built and unusually fluffy, with a silver quality to his coat.

"He's pretty," Berkeley agreed, "and I love sables."

So did Sissy, but an appalling number of people

wanted black-and-tan puppies. What people didn't realize was that *most* German shepherds were sable. The black-and-tan color was recessive.

She sat on the lawn near Berkeley, and Dark Blue Boy turned his attentions to her. He was a big puppy and promptly sat in her lap, as though to claim ownership. Sissy gazed into his face, remembering a time when making these dogs behave immaculately had been the center of her being.

What had gone wrong? She'd branched out into one activity after another, writing plays, acting, teaching. And when she'd been engaged to Clark, she'd been focused on the dogs. Entirely.

Elijah was what had changed her, making mandates about how dogs should be raised. Elijah was right that praise was important in training dogs, but earning their respect was essential, and affection was not the same as respect. *Look at coyotes and wolves,* she thought. She remembered reading about subordinate wolves sneaking food from the dominant animals.

Who really knew what dogs wanted, what their agenda was?

Elijah wants to know, she thought. As her father had.

Then, without deriding herself for anthropomorphic ideas, she gazed at Dark Blue Boy and thought, *This one wants to be in charge.* It was an interesting thought.

"What do you think of the Koehler method?" she abruptly asked Berkeley. Unlike Clark, Berkeley had a fair amount of experience training big dogs.

Berkeley made a wry face. "Well, it has fallen a bit out of favor as cruel, and certainly some of the things he recommends I would never consider doing to my dogs. But his basis for training, his way of getting a dog's attention and keeping it has worked for me. You don't use his system, do you?"

"We used to train all our dogs that way," Sissy admitted, "and, Berkeley, I would get, like, 198s in Open."

Berkeley gave her a sympathetic, almost sisterly, smile. "And then you married a nice man who thought it was cruel?"

"Not exactly. Elijah's realistic. Of course, we never hit our dogs—"

"A good rule," Berkeley agreed. "Especially since I've never been sure it means more to them than that their trainer is going off the deep end, which isn't exactly going to make them confident in their choices."

"I want to check on Eddy again," Sissy said. "I'm sorry."

"Can I see her?" Berkeley asked.

"Sure. Come on. She's probably awake."

Fifteen minutes later, it was clear to Sissy that although Berkeley was excited about getting a new German shepherd puppy, she would *love* to have a baby.

"We're *trying,*" she admitted to Sissy in a hushed tone as the two women sat on the deck, Berkeley holding Eddy, while Clark, across the lawn, continued to scrutinize puppies. "It just seems like it's taking forever. It's as if, when you don't want to be pregnant it's a problem, and now I *do* want children, and it's certainly not happening automatically."

Sissy thought of Ezra. Well, Berkeley wanted a baby of her own, and Ezra wouldn't fill that bill. And, good grief, didn't Elijah realize how upsetting it would be for Ezra to learn the truth? The boy adored Elijah, looked up to him, loved to go to work with him, wanted to be like him.

In the end, Clark and Berkeley bought Red Boy, and Sissy promised to call the next day to see how the puppy was settling into his new home. It had been nice to have Berkeley to talk with. Besides Kennedy and her old friend Allie Morgan, Sissy had few friends these days; she was too busy, too focused on her own family, her own home, her own affairs.

She went into the room she used as a sewing room and office and plucked several dog training books off the shelves. Sitting on the couch with her usual huge jar of water, she nursed Eddy while rereading a book by Barbara Handler. But what consumed her thoughts was Elijah—and Ezra.

Elijah was easy to get along with on the surface, but when he wanted something his way, he seemed to get it. And this business with telling Clark and Ezra the truth of Ezra's paternity might turn out to be one of those things.

She heard the car pull up outside, and Ezra banged in, saying, "Hi, Dark Blue Boy. Mom, I got a hole in one!"

Gene and Elijah followed, Gene with his nose in a book, carrying a jar containing a few insects. Without speaking to Sissy, he continued to his room. She thought about what Elijah had said, the possibility of Gene having a kind of autism. He certainly seemed lacking in social awareness, which sometimes hurt, though she knew she shouldn't take it personally.

"They took Red Boy," Sissy told Elijah.

"Good," he answered. "We can keep Pink Girl. A pretty black-and-tan bitch. Good for the kennel." He showed no sign of any interest in Clark and Berkeley themselves, or in Sissy's feelings about Ezra being Clark's biological son. Of course, he wouldn't in front of Ezra.

He'll insist on having his way on this, Sissy thought. And Elijah would get what he wanted by being remote—pleasant and remote. She would feel his subtle disapproval, and eventually she would yield.

The aggravating man.

When Gene and Ezra had gone outside to do their chores, Sissy stared defiantly at Elijah, waiting for him to bring up the subject.

Instead, he reached for Eddy, held her and kissed her, then bent down to kiss Sissy, too.

She whispered, "Elijah, can we just let it go?"

He sat down on the couch beside her. "It really goes against the grain with me, Sissy. I'm not ashamed that he's not my biological child, and you shouldn't be, either."

"What makes you think I'm *ashamed?*"

"Nothing else makes sense. I think you fear Ezra's reaction."

Sissy stilled her tongue. This accusation hit a little close to the bone. "Well," she admitted, "I do."

"Sissy, I won't let him be disrespectful to you."

"But see, even by saying that, you're admitting there's a reason he *should* be disrespectful."

Elijah shook his head. "I didn't mean that at all."

"I just want you to seriously imagine how you would have felt if, when Ezra was born, I'd told you I was pretty sure he was Clark's child."

"You could have told me before that, Sissy."

"Just answer me," she said.

Elijah sat quietly, holding Eddy. "I would have been hurt."

"And I didn't *want* to hurt you."

"Why didn't you tell me earlier?"

"Because I thought he might be yours." Sissy knew that was a lie. "All right, I thought there might be one chance in a hundred he was yours, but I was willing to pray for that chance and wait. I knew the whole situation would be painful to you."

"And you thought I wouldn't love you anymore."

"Right," she agreed. "Not the same way. So you tell me that you would have loved me the same way. See if you can say that, Elijah."

He hesitated, wondering if he'd begun to love her differently when he finally *had* learned the truth. Yes, he had. But he hadn't loved her less. "Sissy, I wouldn't have loved you the same way. I *don't* love you the same way. But isn't it better that I love who you actually are than a fantasy you've created? I don't need to live in a bubble. My God, you shouldn't have to protect me from something like that."

Sissy listened, playing back every word in her head. So he did love her differently. But he loved her, he claimed, loved her still.

"So you're not *in* love with me," she said.

"I didn't say that!"

She waited for him to continue.

"I love you more, because I know who you really are," he told her. "This is real. We have problems. Good God, we've had overdrafts at the bank. We disagree sometimes. And Ezra's not my biological son. But you're his mother, and I love you both."

Sissy tried to relax, consciously tried to loosen every knot in her muscles. Wasn't this what she'd wanted to hear from the first? She *would* have told him the truth when they first married if she'd been confident of receiving this answer.

No. No this wasn't quite true. *I love you more, because I know who you really are.* "I've always been the same person," she snapped. "You're the one who couldn't see. It's not a fantasy *I* created. It's one you created."

Elijah heard her, understood, knew he had been too willing to be lied to. "That's fair. We share responsibility for the situation. But we need to tell Clark, Sissy. Depending on how he feels, we then may need to tell Ezra."

"Not everything that goes on in this family is your sole decision, Elijah."

"Sissy, it's the right thing to do."

"You don't know that."

Elijah considered. He decided he did know. He considered saying, *If you don't tell him, I will.* Instead, he said, "I don't want to be part of keeping it a secret from him, Sissy."

"You already have been."

Because he'd known the truth about Ezra for months and done nothing. "I don't want to be part of it anymore," he said clearly, calmly, patiently.

"Fine. Don't be."

Elijah didn't understand her. "You want me to tell him?"

"I want you to care a little more about the people you live with than nebulous principles of right and wrong."

The word *nebulous* was well-chosen. The woman could argue. So Elijah said, "I wish my feelings about this were nebulous." He imagined telling Clark what Sissy had kept from him and knew he couldn't do it. She had to be the one, or at least he must do it with her consent.

Tears sprang from her eyes. "I'll tell him, you asshole," she said. "And you'll find out it's not the great solution you think it is."

Elijah knew better than to try to touch her. "I'm sorry if I hurt you."

"Go away. Just go away."

He did.

September 21, 1979

IT TOOK SISSY TIME to work up the courage to call Clark. The anguish of the situation did nothing to increase her love for Elijah. In fact, she sometimes told herself that he was destroying her love by insisting that she reveal the truth to Clark.

It was a Friday when she decided to make the call, the same Friday that Elijah and Gene were meeting with a specialist after school. Her uneasiness about what they might learn somehow offset her having to speak to Clark.

She called him at his and Berkeley's kennels. Clark and Berkeley were rare among handlers. Their training business and sales of training equipment and handling at shows made it possible for them to live comfortably without having to do outside work.

Berkeley answered the phone, and Sissy first spoke to her about Red Boy, inquiring after the puppy. All was well. He was happy and beautiful. Then Sissy said, "I just wanted to speak to Clark briefly. I had a question someone asked me to pass on."

"Sure."

Sissy hated starting things that way, because no doubt Berkeley would soon learn the truth about the reason for her call.

"Hi, Sissy," Clark greeted her.

She swallowed. Sitting on the couch, she gazed out at the lake. "Clark, I really don't know how to say this, but Elijah and I have decided you need to know."

She felt the wariness on the line and attributed it to possible worries about the puppy, unknown genetic troubles, something like that. "My...our... oldest son, Ezra, is your biological son."

Dead silence. Sissy let it be.

Finally he spoke. "I see."

"I'm sorry not to mention it till now. I didn't plan to tell you at all, but Elijah..." She realized she was digging herself in deeper, making a worse impression every moment. She waited, then said, "So...now you know."

Clark said, "Does the boy know?"

"Well, we're waiting to...hear your reaction, I suppose."

"This...Ezra. You know, I looked at him once and thought he looked like my sister's son. I thought nothing of it. What?" Sissy heard Berkeley in the background, asking some question. Clark said, "Look, I need to discuss this with Berkeley, but if you're wondering if I want to be part of his life, I think the answer is yes. If— if it won't be detrimental to him."

How could it not be? Sissy wanted to demand. Elijah and now Clark seemed to think Ezra would simply take it in stride that the man he'd always called Dad was not his father.

Sissy kept her tone discouraging. "If you insist."

More silence. Clark said at last, "We'll call you later about this."

"All right," Sissy agreed. "We won't do anything until we hear from you."

"THE DOCTOR SAID he's a high-functioning autistic. He thinks it's something they're beginning to call after a man named Asperger. Anyhow, there's nothing to be done. With medication, at least."

Sissy stared at Elijah. "So what does this mean? Now he's handicapped and won't have a normal life?"

Elijah shook his head, whether in agreement or not she couldn't tell. "It's just something he has to work his way around. Like all of us do with different things." He had brought her photocopies of sections about Asperger's from textbooks in the library. He had given Gene copies as well. "He's very bright, as we knew."

"Well, this thing he has about no one touching him—does this mean he'll never be able to get married or even live on his own?"

"Let's not map his future out for him as less wonderful than it can be. Our job is to work with his teachers and make school manageable for him, help him to form the kind of relationships of which he's capable."

"With scorpions?" Sissy said.

Elijah gave her a rueful smile. "With people."

Sissy made herself take slow, deep breaths. "I'm sorry," she told him. "It's been a hard day. I talked to Clark."

"Ah." A pause. "What did he say?"

"He wants to know him, he thinks, but he hasn't talked to Berkeley about it. She may have different ideas."

Elijah considered this. "Thank you," he said.

"Yes, well." Sissy saw Eddy begin to stir on the bed, and she picked up the baby. She proceeded to ignore Elijah, speaking to Eddy instead. "You're wet, aren't you, sweetheart?"

November 22, 1979

BY THANKSGIVING DAY, they still had not heard back from Clark and Berkeley. That morning, Sissy told Elijah tartly, "So it didn't make any difference at all. It was unnecessary to tell him."

Elijah bit his tongue before he could say that Sissy was reminding him more of her mother every day. Instead, he told himself that Sissy was under exceptional stress.

For the first time since her father's death, Heloise Atherton was coming to the house. It was to be a family Thanksgiving gathering—Kennedy's idea—and she had literally begged Sissy to at least *invite* their mother. Surprisingly Heloise had accepted.

"Which means the house has to be twenty times cleaner and everyone has to be immaculately behaved!" Sissy had told Elijah.

"Don't worry," he'd said. "We'll pitch in and help." By which he'd meant that he and Ezra would help with the housework, and he would take care of Eddy. Kennedy was arriving at noon to help with the cooking. She and her family would be staying with Sissy's mother.

Late in the morning, Elijah persuaded Gene to help clean the kennels. Sissy was not sure how he managed to do it. Elijah left the boy to it and came back inside. Sissy said, "Is he really cleaning the kennel?"

"Yes. It's Oak's, and he said he would do it if he was the only one allowed to keep it clean, and I said it was a deal."

"Only if he does a good enough job," Sissy warned.

"I think he will. I think he wants to be able to control the area."

Soon after, they heard Kennedy's car outside,

and she and Gerry came in with their two daughters Ellen and Jessica.

Gene came inside after the family. He looked at them and said, "You're getting fat, Aunt Kennedy."

Sissy shut her eyes, opened them and considered infanticide. "Go to your room," she said.

Gene looked puzzled and angry.

Kennedy, who indeed had gained some weight since her second pregnancy, steadied her wavering chin and set down toddler Jessica, whom she had carried inside.

Elijah said, "Let's go to your room, Gene."

In Gene's room, he sat on his son's bed.

"Why did I have to come in here?" Gene asked. "It wasn't a lie."

Gene never lied. His mind didn't work that way.

"It hurt Aunt Kennedy's feelings."

Gene stared at Elijah, he couldn't comprehend what Elijah was saying.

"So I'd like you to say that you're sorry."

Gene didn't answer. Instead, he went to look at one of his scorpions in its plastic homemade terrarium. "I have two female scorpions," he said.

Elijah said, "I'm talking about your aunt's feelings, Gene. Do you like to have your feelings hurt?"

"I thought there were three females, but there are only two."

Elijah said, "I would like you to please tell Aunt Kennedy that you're sorry."

"Her feelings will still be hurt," Gene said matter-of-factly.

An astute remark—and on the subject. "Nonetheless. Or…you could say something nice to her."

This possibility seemed beyond Gene.

Elijah said, "Can you think about that?"

Gene said, "Only scorpions have pectines. They're mechanoreceptors and contact chemoreceptors."

Elijah felt abruptly exhausted. Gene would talk about scorpions on and on. *How can I teach him to get along with people?*

The most intransigent dog-training problem he could imagine seemed simple in comparison.

HELOISE ATHERTON LOOKED at the railing on the deck and sniffed. "This is rather nice. Who did it for you?"

"Elijah did it," Sissy told her mother. Every fiber of her being was tense.

Heloise said nothing. Gene had come outside carrying two pillows. There'd been no snow yet this year, and Elijah had left the furniture out. Now Gene sat on one of the wood deck chairs with pillows strangely covering him and read the telephone book. Sissy wanted to protect Gene from any barbs Heloise might throw at him. On the other hand, Gene seemed impervious to most cruel remarks.

Heloise did seem to be staring at Gene critically, but all she said was, "My brother used to do that."

"Read the phone book?" asked Sissy.

"No," replied Heloise. "The pillows."

Sissy blinked at her mother, who hadn't sounded condemnatory. Tolerance of Gene's eccentricities was the last thing she'd expected. "Uncle John?" she asked.

Her mother shook his head. "Timothy."

Uncle Timothy, the strange uncle whom Sissy had never met. Uncle Timothy lived alone, and her mother and Uncle John paid to have a woman come in and clean.

"But he's an engineer," Sissy said, then realized she'd revealed too much of her fears for Gene.

"Of course he is. Maybe your child will be, too."

"Gene," Sissy supplied, supposing that her mother had forgotten his name.

"Yes, I know," Heloise said and turned away.

Sissy made herself speak. "He has Asperger's, some kind of autism."

Gene did not look up, and she cursed herself for speaking of him as though he wasn't present.

"Nonsense," said her mother.

Gene never looked up, just continued reading the phone book.

Kennedy's husband, Gerry, came outside, stood behind Gene's chair, reached down and ruffled his hair. "How are you doing, buddy?"

Gene squirmed away, took his phone books and pillows, and went toward the dog kennels.

Gerry gave Sissy an apologetic look. "I forgot he hates to be touched."

"There are a lot of people here," she said, "for him."

Her mother gazed after Gene, watching him open one of the kennels, step inside and close it behind him.

GENE EMERGED from the kennel to join the rest of the family at the dinner table late that afternoon. He brought a book about scorpions to the dinner table. Elijah asked him to put it away while they ate. Gene put it in his lap and covered it with a napkin. After everyone filled their plates and grace was said, Ezra talked with Gerry about his science class in school. Gene butted in to tell nearly everything he knew about scorpions. Gerry asked Ezra a question about his studies, and Gene talked above Ezra about scorpions.

Both Sissy and Elijah urged him to let Ezra speak.

Gene climbed down from his chair, took his book and walked away from the table in robotic fashion. A bit later, he went outside to the kennels again with his blanket and pillows.

Sissy thought briefly about Ezra, about the fact he was Clark's son and they still didn't know if Clark wanted anything to do with him. Had Clark told Berkeley? Did Berkeley object to Clark's having a relationship with Ezra? She imagined telling her mother the truth someday and wanted to groan aloud. Instead, she offered the cranberry sauce around again.

THE LIGHTS WERE OFF in the kennels when Heloise Atherton opened the gate, in search of her grandson Gene. She found him in the doghouse, pillows piled on top of him, with his blanket. He was reading with a penlight.

She looked at him, remembering her brother Timothy at that age, remembering long-ago things, her mother screaming that there was nothing to be done with him. Timothy had liked Heloise. He'd come up with crazy schemes, antics, like making dummies and placing them in surprising places in the house. She sat down on the cold concrete, which was as immaculate as the concrete in her own kennels. She said, "What do you like to do?"

Gene sat up. "I like scorpions. Would you like to see my scorpions? I'm going to earn money and buy a tarantula."

CHAPTER TEN

The dogs have favorite songs and favorite artists. Louis Armstrong was a favorite with Teddy, while his daughter Martha seemed to be a Joni Mitchell fan, always emerging from wherever she'd been to come into the room when she heard *Both Sides Now* played on the stereo.

—*Crossover Language,* Elijah Workman,
1990

June 4, 1981

CLARK NEVER PHONED, and when Elijah saw him at a dog show more than a year later, Clark gave a shake of his head which seemed to say, *I'm letting it go.* And both Sissy and Elijah had noticed that Berkeley seemed not to want Clark to talk to them anymore.

So long had passed since they'd heard from him that Elijah, like Sissy, had begun to accept that Clark had decided to leave things with Ezra as they were. Nonetheless, for Elijah, telling Clark the truth about Ezra had eased his mind a bit, and he'd started to believe Sissy's explanation that she hadn't told the truth from the start because she'd been afraid of losing his love.

Also, he'd begun to wonder whether it really would be the best thing for Ezra to know about Clark. Ezra was well-adjusted, the model oldest child, polite and cooperative at school, smart, handsome.

In the past months, Gene had changed, too. At first, when Sissy and Elijah had seen signs that Gene was beginning to learn how to make appropriate responses to people, to learn a minimum of social normalcy, they'd been pleased. But Elijah had also noticed that his being more comfortable with people, which would never save him from being considered a nerd and wouldn't stop him from repetitive behaviors like twirling his pencils or hopping on one leg for extended periods, had been accompanied by an alarming awareness of the way the minds of others worked. He seemed to understand their fears, which had begun to result in frequent conflicts between him and Ezra.

Ezra was afraid of scorpions, spiders and centipedes, all of which Gene liked. Gene also knew what would upset his older brother and almost arranged for such things to happen. Elijah discovered quite by accident that Gene was blackmailing his brother out of his allowance by threatening to tell everyone at school about the time that Ezra had wet his pants in the Christmas pageant. Gene put a large slug on Ezra's chair at the breakfast table, and Ezra sat down without looking.

Sissy had told Elijah that she worried that their younger son was becoming a sociopath. Elijah had begun to feel uneasy about the pranks that Gene found funny. There was nothing Elijah could do but take away privileges. Gene was forced to pay Ezra his own allowance for the length of time he'd blackmailed Ezra. Grounding him was not particularly meaningful, as Gene had few friends, other than just one other boy who was interested in computers and chemistry.

One Wednesday evening early in June, when Gene had gone out on his bicycle, which he'd just learned to ride the month before, Elijah paused at the door to his room, planning to close it to improve the air-conditioner's effectiveness. He glanced inside curiously, seeing the usual immaculate order. Gene always put things down in his room in exactly the same place from where he'd picked them up. He emptied his own waste-basket each evening before bed.

It was the wastebasket which caught Elijah's eye.

It was nearly overflowing because Gene hadn't yet emptied it. He must have been busy with paper today, and Elijah stepped in to glance in the trash bin, hoping to see that Gene had been working quadratic equations or continuing his study of chemistry, things which fascinated him already, when his classmates were still learning long division.

Instead, Elijah caught sight of a half-crumpled note written in Gene's untidy scrawl, amidst magazine pages with shapes cut out.

No, not shapes. Letters.

What Elijah could read of the writing said, *If you want the negatives of you and Mrs. McCormick, put 100 USD—*

If Elijah had never heard of Mrs. McCormick he might have dismissed this as part of some game. But Mrs. McCormick, the whole neigh-borhood suspected, needed less constant atten-tion than she was receiving from the minister who stopped by her house most weekday afternoons. So Sissy said. And Gene did own a camera, an in-expensive point-and-shoot instamatic.

Elijah imagined telling Sissy that Gene had moved on to blackmailing adults. He peered around Gene's desk, looking for the photographs, but he found none. Gene had been unusually sloppy in letting his note be found.

The phone rang, and Elijah, who was alone in the house because Ezra was at a Cub Scout meeting and Sissy had taken Eddy to the grocery store, went to answer it.

"Elijah, it's Clark." When Elijah didn't answer immediately, Clark clarified, "Clark Treffinger-Hart."

Elijah tensed slightly but made his voice warm. "Hello, Clark. Good to hear from you."

"You must think the worst of me." When Elijah didn't immediately respond, he added, "Not doing anything about Ezra. You know."

"I don't feel that way," Elijah said, but admitted, "I did wonder if there were problems with your wife. If perhaps she wanted your lives to stay as they were."

"That sums it up," Clark said, "but it's no longer an issue. Well, I shouldn't say that. We've recently adopted an eight-month-old baby, and it has changed her feelings. She believes she can love Ezra as much as she does Anne—that's our baby."

Elijah thought this over. "I can see it would make a difference."

"Does Ezra know? That I'm his biological father?"

"No," Elijah replied. "Not yet. But I guess that's the next thing to do."

But, in fact, the next thing was to tell Sissy.

SISSY STARED at the bulletin board outside the market. She had just rearranged all the flyers to make room for her own.

TRAIN YOUR DOG THIS SUMMER
CLASSES IN OBEDIENCE, AGILITY,
RALLY & BREED

Elijah wasn't happy with her decision to quit her job at the high school to return to training dogs full-time. He hadn't liked her explanation that she felt her life had been too unfocused, that she needed to devote herself completely and entirely to dogs. Her quitting teaching drama meant giving up valuable benefits as a drama and speech teacher. Elijah's at the Humane Society were not nearly as good.

But she wanted to be more available to the children, especially Eddy, but also—for what help it might offer—Gene. It was possible that she and Elijah would have no more children. She didn't want to miss any more time with those she had.

Sissy pushed Eddy and her groceries to the car.

She unloaded the groceries into the back of the used Volvo station wagon, plucked Eddy from the cart and happened to glance across the lot.

Her eyes met her mother's at the same time, and Sissy waved. "There's Grandma El." It was what Eddy called Heloise Atherton.

Heloise had just gotten out of her Buick; she locked the car and hurried to her daughter.

Since the Thanksgiving Heloise had come to the lakefront house, things had improved between them. For some reason, Heloise particularly liked Gene. This was the last thing Sissy would have expected, but it pleased her, despite Gene's often diabolical behavior.

Her mother said crisply, "Hello, Kennedy. Hello, Sissy."

"Hi, Mom."

"How's your bitch?"

Sissy knew her mother meant Julia and was touched that she'd asked. But Sissy could not speak. Tears sprang to her eyes. "We put her down." Julia was buried with Teddy and Whiteout in the cemetery they'd created on the hilly area farthest from the lake.

Heloise nodded curtly.

Sissy composed herself, glanced at her mother and realized that Heloise seemed tense and preoccupied.

"Is something wrong?" Sissy asked.

"No," her mother snapped.

Sissy had the distinct feeling that Heloise wanted to say something to her, but for some reason was holding off. Her mother was sixty-seven now and not the strong woman she'd once been. She'd seemed to grow thin and brittle with the years. Sissy often wondered how she coped alone with the demands of running a German shepherd kennel. Shepherds were large dogs, strong. Heloise no longer showed them herself in Breed, could not run fast enough in the ring.

Sissy reflected now that her mother had also been nicer to Elijah since she'd taken to Gene. And abruptly, for the first time in years, she felt sorry for Heloise. "Are you managing all right with the kennels, Mom?"

"Of course," snapped her mother, making Sissy regret she'd said anything. "I have an assistant. Actually," she added, "I wanted to ask your Gene if he'd like the chance to earn some money. He could be a help. I see what a good job he does with your sable's kennel run."

Sissy had more than one sable, but knew that Heloise meant Oak, arguably the finest dog Sissy had. Thinking of Gene's typical methods of "earning money"—blackmailing his brother, pretending to collect for the "Echo Springs

Children's Project" (a charity of his own creation whose beneficiary was Gene Workman)—Sissy wondered if helping his grandmother would appeal. Caring for Oak's kennel was one of his chores, and he did it with pride and a certain possessiveness.

She suggested, "Why don't you call him on the phone and ask him?"

"I think I may," Heloise replied and gazed critically at Eddy. "Well, none of your children are bad-looking, Sissy," she said at last. "I suppose I'll see you next weekend."

There was a show in Des Moines.

"Yes," Sissy said. "I'd like to have Elijah there, but someone needs to stay home with Gene."

"He's been going to shows all his life," objected Heloise.

"He doesn't like traveling," Sissy replied. And Gene had begun behaving so bizarrely at shows that Sissy found herself embarrassed. Everyone must wonder what she and Elijah were doing to him to make him act that way. When she'd told Elijah that, he'd said that people should be more sensitive and tolerant.

Her mother said, "My mother never liked Timothy because he wasn't affectionate with her."

Sissy opened her mouth to say that of course she liked Gene, if her mother was implying that she did not. Her mother hadn't sounded sympathetic to anyone, just matter-of-fact.

Sissy pressed her lips tightly together and said, "Well, we need to get home."

GENE RODE RESENTFULLY in the car beside his father to retrieve the note from Reverend Marshall's house. Gene had pushed it through the mailbox, and he didn't see why his father couldn't simply call the Reverend and tell him he didn't have to pay the money.

Gene resented the whole thing because when he'd blackmailed Ezra, his mother had told him indignantly that wetting his pants was something Ezra had not been able to help at the time, and that it was wrong to take advantage of people like that.

Gene had asked his father whether there was some reason Reverend Marshall couldn't help carrying on with someone's wife.

His father said that wasn't the case but that it was wrong—and illegal—to blackmail people. But Gene needed money, so now he was going to have to think of a new way to get some. His mother had said she would pay him for pulling weeds, five cents a weed. That, in Gene's opinion, was extremely cheap—worker mistreatment—so he'd decided to rip the weeds in two to double the money he could get out of them. But it still wasn't enough.

What Gene wanted was his own business, and he knew what kind. He would breed and sell arachnids. There were businesses devoted to selling tarantulas, for instance. Less money in scorpions unfortunately, but centipedes might be good. And he needed money to purchase breeding stock. But his parents kept taking away his allowance.

The preacher lived alone, and his car was in front of the rectory when they drove up.

Elijah said, "Let's go."

"No," said Gene.

Elijah took a deep breath. He'd had time to think about this. "Okay," he said. "You have a choice. We can go up there, and you can tell the Reverend to disregard the note he received, or there's an alternative. *I* will talk to the man. Then, when we return home, you will get a taste of what it's like to be in jail."

"You'll ground me?" asked Gene.

There was no inflection in his voice, but Elijah sensed his interest.

"No," Elijah replied. "What you have done— twice now—is illegal. I told you earlier when you blackmailed your brother that it's against the law."

"No, it's not."

Elijah looked at him.

"You blackmail Mother all the time if she's acting in a way you don't like. You ignore her."

Elijah was amazed at the sophistication of this statement from someone whose emotions were supposed to be so different from everyone else's. "In those instances, I'm not blackmailing your mother. I'm angry. That's the best I can...do about it."

Turning off the engine at the curb, he glanced at his son. Gene seemed to be thinking over what he'd said.

"In any case," Elijah continued, "it's not an acceptable way to earn money. So—your experience in 'jail' will not be like being grounded. Your pets, books and possessions will be removed from your room and you'll be confined there. Your mother or I or Ezra will take over your jobs—cleaning Oak's kennel, for instance. People in jail are not allowed to keep their jobs on the outside." He looked at Gene. "Which is it to be?"

Gene opened his car door.

Elijah hid his relief, then decided that revealing his own feelings wouldn't matter. Gene was only thinking of his own situation and what would be most uncomfortable for him.

"HE SAID," Elijah told Sissy late that evening in their bedroom, "and I quote, 'My father explained to me that it's wrong to blackmail people, so you don't have to pay the money.'"

Sissy closed her eyes. "And he'd already gotten the note?"

"Oh, yes," said Elijah.

Carry jumped up on the bed. Carry, formerly Pink Girl, had earned her name by carrying things around in her mouth. She was the most promising puppy yet to come out of Genesis lines. She was black-and-tan, short-backed with a very nice croup and excellent side gait. She was also a clown. Virtually everything had potential as a toy where Carry was concerned.

Sissy told her, "Off," and made sure she got down from the bed. "What about these photographs?"

"Gene gave them to me, and I've destroyed them and the negatives."

"You didn't give them back to the minister?"

"He didn't believe they existed. Neither of us enlightened him."

Sissy covered her face with her hands. "He'll end up in jail."

She meant Gene, Elijah knew.

"I doubt it," Elijah said.

Hearing the certainty in his voice, Sissy decided not to argue but to let herself be soothed. She lay down in bed and pulled the covers over her, reaching for a new dog-training book on her nightstand.

She heard Elijah sigh as he climbed into bed beside her.

She glanced over at him to find him staring at the ceiling. "Clark called."

THE NEXT DAY was Friday. Heloise Atherton had phoned the night before, spoken to Gene and gotten his agreement to come to her house in the morning and help with her kennels. She would pick him up.

Ezra was in a hurry to go to a friend's house, and Sissy and Elijah had manufactured chores to keep him at home until Gene had left with his grandmother.

Then, with Eddy having a tea party with her stuffed animals in her bedroom, Sissy said, "Ezra, Daddy and I have to talk to you."

Ezra threw a glance at Elijah as though wondering what he could have done to earn a "talking to."

Elijah looked at Sissy, saw the anguish on her face. He realized he'd never seen her do anything so brave as what she was about to do. He saw she did not want to hurt Ezra, didn't want to risk her son's anger toward her, but she was determined now. Last night she hadn't even bothered to argue, had simply sighed and said, *Then we must tell him.*

At least Ezra and Gene knew "the facts of life," Elijah having imparted these things during a dog breeding three years earlier.

Gene had said matter-of-factly, "I already knew that," had further imparted that male snakes had two hemipenises, had described copulation in scorpions and tarantulas, and had walked away.

Ezra had simply looked appalled.

Elijah sat down on the couch beside Sissy, with Ezra in a nearby chair, looking in a hurry to spring up and go kick his soccer ball with his friends.

Sissy said, "Ezra, your dad—your dad isn't your biological father."

Ezra's eyes rounded.

Elijah's thoughts shot to Gene. He could well imagine Gene taunting Ezra, telling him he was adopted. Strange, in his own family, Elijah had been very much the leader, but Ezra, the eldest in this family, was constantly at the mercy of Gene.

Ezra said, "I'm adopted?"

"No," both his parents said as one, and Elijah saw in Sissy's eyes that she'd been imagining the same scenario that he had. Rarely had he felt so utterly in sync with his wife. They knew their children.

Sissy said, "I was engaged to be married before

I met your father, and I…was intimate with that man. You are his son."

Ezra gazed in disbelief at his parents.

"But you'll *always* be my son," Elijah interjected quickly. "I couldn't love you any more than I do."

He said, "You lied to me. You both lied to me."

Elijah felt the words to his soul. It was true. Sissy had gone white.

Sissy rushed over it. "Your…biological father…he wants to know you. To spend time with you."

"Are you giving me to him?" Ezra demanded.

"No!" Elijah exclaimed. "My name's on your birth certificate. You're my son."

"Right," said Ezra with acrid sarcasm.

Elijah hardly knew how to respond.

Sissy said, "Ezra, we *love* you."

"Right," Ezra repeated in the same voice. Then, "So who is he? That Clark guy?"

Of course. The kids knew that Sissy had been engaged to someone else before she'd married Ezra. In fact, prior to learning the truth about Ezra's parentage, Elijah had blithely told them the story about taking Sissy away from the cathedral. They hadn't formally met Clark because the boys had been away from home when Clark and Berkeley had picked their puppy, whom they'd called Oxford.

"Yes," Sissy was the one to say. "Clark Treffinger-Hart. He's a nice man, and he wants to know you, Ezra. He'd like to spend some time with you, if you're willing."

"Why?" said Ezra, reminding Elijah irresistibly of Gene.

"Because you're his son," said Sissy. "You're his flesh and blood, and he wants to know you."

Ezra seemed to think this over. He shrugged. "All right. Can I go to Jack's now?"

Elijah saw Sissy's shoulders relax. He thought how incredibly beautiful she was. At thirty-seven, she looked much as she had at twenty-five, and he knew other men found her attractive, too.

"Are you okay?" Sissy asked Ezra.

"Sure," he said, sounding not right at all.

They watched him collect his bike helmet—something he hated but which Elijah insisted upon—and go out the back door.

Sissy whispered, almost to herself, "This is just the beginning. Everything will be different now."

"Different," Elijah agreed. "Not necessarily worse."

She didn't bother to answer.

CHAPTER ELEVEN

Though Whiteout was the larger dog, he accepted Teddy as alpha. He never showed any human the same respect he did the younger, intact German shepherd.

—*Dog Brethren,* Elijah Workman, 1977

April 10, 1984

"I'M GOING TO LEAVE Elijah," Sissy announced to Allie Morgan, with whom she was having juice in the country club bar after a round of tennis. It was a Wednesday afternoon, uncommonly warm for that time of year.

Allie looked shocked. "Why?"

Sissy regretted her confession. "Forget it. I shouldn't have said anything. I'm just talking."

Allie drank her own juice. Finally she ventured, "You can talk. I'm glad to listen. Marriage is tough. God, I know it."

But Sissy knew she couldn't explain everything

to Allie. Sissy had three children with Elijah. He didn't beat her, wasn't a drunk or a drug addict, held down a job. In short, what could she have to complain about?

"Allie, I've been in love with him since I was twelve years old, and—well, you know about Ezra. He has never loved me the same since he found out about that."

"He loves you, Sissy," Allie said with such firmness that Sissy doubted her own observations. "Look, you guys have been married a long time. And he's not...I don't know. He's a man. Men don't express their emotions the way we do."

Now that she'd started, Sissy couldn't stop. "He loves Gene more than he loves any of the rest of us. And he has no sympathy for *my* feelings when it comes to what Gene wants and needs. Ezra and Eddy and I all hate scorpions, and Elijah is letting Gene *breed* them and sell them to pet shops and collectors."

Allie shuddered sympathetically.

"Then, the other day, Gene came home with this ten-inch long centipede. First, he tries to tell us it's native, and I said, 'I don't care. Get rid of it.' Elijah didn't believe it, and it turns out the thing's from Malaysia or somewhere, and I think it's somewhat venomous."

Allie was looking properly horrified, perhaps

wondering if her youngest should be allowed to visit the Workmans and play with Eddy.

"In any case, it's violent, ferocious and I'm terrified of it. It eats *live mice.* But Gene has heavy-duty gloves, and he said my mother helped him order it, which turns out to be true. He promised to keep its terrarium locked, and Elijah agreed, and now we're living with *Rover.*"

Allie couldn't resist. "So you're really leaving the centipede, not Elijah."

"Oh, shut up. Want me to bring it to your house?"

"No, I do not. Have you told Elijah how strongly you feel?"

"He says Gene is very responsible and won't let it escape. I don't care! I don't want the thing in the house."

Allie said, "But you say you're in love with Elijah."

"Not anymore. He has killed my love. Actively killed it. He's aloof to me, lets the kids run wild— *especially* Gene, who needs discipline more than any thirteen-year-old in Missouri—and he's actually quite dictatorial. He always has been. I can see you think I'm crazy."

"No," Allie answered, nonetheless sounding doubtful.

Sissy barely heard. She was unhappy. Did it

really matter why? She was immersing herself thoroughly in the kennel, and had seen Clark and Berkeley take Oxford to the Eukanuba show, with excellent result. Westminster really seemed like something Sissy might achieve.

But there was something she wanted, something she was reluctant to ask for.

Her mother had produced a miracle of a bitch called Delilah, and Sissy wanted her mother to breed Delilah to Oxford, and she wanted a puppy from that breeding, but she owned neither of the dogs involved. Her mother, for all her gratitude in having Gene work for her, for all her improved attitude toward Elijah, had never forgiven Sissy entirely for leaving Clark at the altar, thus embarrassing her, nor for taking Teddy away from her parents' kennel. And she had said that she was not interested in breeding to any dog out of Sissy's lines.

It was *so stupid*. But Elijah had said, annoyingly, "It's the same thing you said when you started Genesis. You didn't want anything to do with her lines."

Now Allie said, "You don't want advice, do you." It wasn't a question but an observation.

Sissy looked at her. "Say it."

"Unless there's something you're not telling me, he's a pretty good guy, Sissy. And at work—" Allie was a paralegal "—I've seen the pain of divorce, especially for the kids. Think hard about it. Some things you can't take back."

Sissy felt a darkness in her heart, an ominous sense that she was hearing the truth. If she hurt Elijah by leaving him, he might someday take her back, but it wouldn't make him any more emotionally available. Quite the reverse.

"I do not want to live with that animal," she repeated softly to herself.

"You should tell him that," Allie said. Then she laughed suddenly. "Rover."

"Mom." Gene's face showed little. He was that way, Sissy thought. It was hard to tell what he was feeling, particularly when his voice seemed without intonation, which was most of the time. Still she sensed a certain urgency in him. "Have you seen Rover?"

Sissy had returned from tennis with Allie to find Gene home from school, and Ezra just returned from soccer practice. Eddy was at a friend's house, and Elijah would pick her up on the way home from work in time for supper. Sissy expected them in fifteen minutes or so.

Ezra was stretched out on the couch doing homework. Clark would be taking him to this week's soccer game in Osage Beach. He looked more like his natural father than ever, and he seemed to enjoy being in Clark's and Berkeley's company. Clark spoiled him in a way Elijah didn't like because it meant Ezra was treated differently from Eddy and Gene. In fact, right now, George, Ezra's own German shorthaired pointer lay at his feet in an enforced down stay. George had proven a determined chewer, worse than even Whiteout had been, but Sissy didn't begrudge her eldest son the dog or think Clark's treatment of Ezra would hurt. Sissy thought Gene was treated differently already, and it was natural that Eddy would be, too, because she was the only girl.

Ezra sat up straighter on the couch, and Sissy whirled from the sink, where she was cleaning a pot before cheese could congeal in it. "What do you mean 'Where's Rover?'" she demanded.

Gene shuffled to the door of his room and shuffled back out again, head down, looking at a plastic terrarium with a hole in one bottom corner that looked as though it had been chewed. From the inside out.

Sissy's eyes went wide.

Ezra leaped off the couch, scanning the furniture and floor.

Sissy shut off the water, went to the telephone and opened the phone book.

"What are you doing?" Gene asked.

"Calling the exterminator," his mother told him firmly.

"Mom! You can't do that. Anyhow, they're resistant to pesticides."

"Oh, no they're not," Sissy said, wondering how he expected her to fall for that. She flipped through the Yellow Pages, looking for "Pest Control."

She heard Elijah's car on the gravel outside, and she walked away from the phone to greet her husband and daughter at the door. Kennedy, a winsome four year old, said, "Mama, can I take gymnastics? Daddy said I have to ask you."

"Tumbling," Elijah clarified. "Allie Morgan's daughter is teaching a class starting in May."

"Oh," said Sissy. "Eddy, honey, we'll talk about this later. Go wash your hands for dinner. Gene, come here."

Gene said, "All right, all right. He hasn't escaped. It was a joke."

"What?" Sissy nearly shrieked.

"I keep him in a glass terrarium, Mom, and it's locked. He's in my closet."

"What's this?" said Elijah.

Ezra, instead of going back to sit on the couch, marched into Gene's room.

Gene said, "I don't want him in my room."

Sissy said to Elijah, "The centipede goes. And

I think maybe the rest should, too, because it isn't funny. That animal is venomous enough to—" She stopped herself, because Elijah knew the end of the sentence. To kill Eddy.

To her surprise, Elijah touched her shoulder, putting a calming pressure there, and said, "I agree. I'll take care of this."

INDEED, the centipede was locked in its glass terrarium in Gene's closet, hidden to give the maximum impact to his "joke." Elijah ordered Ezra out of his brother's room and shut the door. He glanced around at the floor-to-ceiling shelves of scorpions and tarantulas. Rover was the only centipede.

Gene sat on his bed but didn't look at his father. This was not unusual.

Elijah said, "You blew it. That centipede is not a subject for jokes. And you didn't just blow it where the centipede is concerned. We're getting rid of all your stock. And I don't want to find you've tried to set it up somewhere else. If, for one year, you can refrain from doing things that you know damn well we don't want you to do—blackmailing people, tormenting your siblings—"

"I don't torment Eddy," Gene said.

Actually, this was true. Gene rather liked his little sister. She, in turn, showed little fear of scorpions and tarantulas, though she hadn't especially liked Rover.

"In any case, if you maintain good behavior for that length of time, then one year from now, you may renew your business. What's more, I'll construct a building in which you can keep your breeding animals and your stock."

Gene shifted his eyes sideways, an unusual move for him. "I bet Grandma would do it now."

"No, she won't," Elijah replied. *Because I'm going to ask her not to.* And he was pretty sure Heloise would listen. When he'd discussed the centipede with her, right after Gene had brought it home, she'd said, *I should have found out more about it, Elijah, but I don't think it's dangerous. the dealer just asked if it was for an experienced keeper, and I said it was.*

"What if Grandma keeps Rover for me for the next year?"

Gene shook his head.

"What if Grandma dies? It was a gift to me. Gifts from grandparents are special."

Elijah was astounded at the depths to which Gene would sink in manipulation—at least he assumed it was manipulation. With Gene, you could never tell. For all Elijah knew, a centipede might be Gene's idea of a precious family heirloom. "The answer is no."

Gene picked up a thick college text on arachnids and arthropods, collected his four-season sleeping bag from his bed and walked out of the room. Elijah knew where he was going. To the kennels.

Nonetheless, Elijah found himself waiting for the other shoe to drop.

THAT NIGHT, in her gratitude, Sissy confessed that she'd actually been thinking of leaving him.

"Because of Rover?" Elijah asked in disbelief, blotting out recent memory, memory to which no one but he had been a part. Horrible memory of the destruction of an animal, of life. Though Gene later had simply emptied his pockets of the things he carried each day—a pencil, two pieces of dental floss, and two eight-sided dice—placed them on his desk exactly where he always did and gotten ready for bed.

"No." She shook her head. "It's just that sometimes I think you love Gene more than the rest of us. Including me."

"That's ridiculous," Elijah said, yet he felt a stab of guilt. A parent shouldn't have a favorite child. For years he'd warred against the fact that Ezra was his favorite. But since he'd met Clark Treffinger-Hart, Ezra had been distancing himself from Elijah, from their whole family, it seemed.

And at some point, even before that, Elijah had begun to feel an even more intense love for Gene, who was simply so much trouble. He'd gone through similar feelings with the dogs before. One would be his favorite for several months, then another.

But did he show so much favoritism to Gene that even Sissy felt insecure in comparison?

She said, "And I think you've never really forgiven me for Ezra and that you never really will forgive me."

"That is definitely untrue," Elijah said. He sat on the end of the bed beside her, looked into her violet eyes beneath her still unlined brow. "I wouldn't hold a grudge like that. It would only make me unhappy."

"You've been aloof ever since you learned about Ezra. I keep thinking it will stop, but it never does."

"Sissy, it's not something I'm doing on purpose. It's just how I am. It's my personality." And she'd been ready to leave him because of it. That shocked him. Elijah sometimes felt as though he'd bent over backward to meet her every desire, and she'd wanted to leave?

"Is it money?" he asked. He'd been trying to write another dog book. The book, in fact, was already sold; he'd received an advance on signing half a year before. It was to be a comparison between three dogs he'd known.

She shook her head. "No. I've told you what it is. I want you to stop being so remote."

A moment later, she stood and began to change for bed, removing jeans and her long-sleeved scoopneck T-shirt and pulling on a T-shirt of Elijah's that skimmed her thighs.

Elijah said, "You are so beautiful. Do you know that?"

Sissy heard him and glanced in the full-length mirror on the back of the door. She saw dimpled thighs, but she also saw a woman who looked reasonably good for her age. She stayed fit, not immaculately so. She sometimes thought of herself as beautiful, and she wondered now if that was because Elijah saw her that way.

When he turned out the light and joined her in bed minutes later, she immediately felt his wanting for her. She hoped for deeper kisses, for more evidence of love.

Elijah pushed away the thought that she'd been considering leaving him. She was so beautiful. He could barely see her in the moonlight through the window. Sometimes they made love with one of the lamps on, sometimes without. Sometimes with condoms, sometimes without, neither especially keen for another child, though Elijah knew that Sissy, like him, would welcome a baby if the event happened.

Was he aloof? Had he truly treated her differently since he'd learned he wasn't Ezra's natural father?

He felt the same desire for her he'd always felt, a desire so ferocious that he curbed it always, needing to be gentle with her. He held her head gently stroking her hair, as they kissed.

Had he really almost lost her?

His tongue touched hers. He felt her breasts press against him, felt her wanting.

"Sissy," he whispered, kissing her cheeks, her fine jaw, her beautiful chin, her throat.

He wanted her so badly, so much. She touched him, drawing him toward her, into her.

One with her, he tried to think how to banish what she called his aloofness even as he felt it rise in him. Part of him knew her as the person who hadn't waited for him for marriage, who was spoiled thanks to a wealthy background, who demanded one thing after another from him and expected her demands to be met. Another part of him knew all those things as his own prejudice, as something wrong in him, to expect anyone to meet his ideal of what was perfect.

She shuddered against him, clinging to him, crying his name.

Afterward, he held her close, her head against his heart, willing himself not to judge her.

Sissy said, "What did you do with Rover?"

Elijah didn't answer immediately. Gene had been in the kennels when Elijah had taken the heavy work gloves, eighteen-inch tongs and Rover's terrarium from his room. He said, "Put him in a Ziploc bag and ran over him with the car." He could picture the headlines: Humane Society Investigator Murders Malaysian Centipede.

Sissy made a sympathetic sound. "Sorry you had to do that."

Elijah said, "I had to do it."

Afterward, he'd done what he should have done when Gene brought the thing home. He'd borrowed one of his son's texts on arthropods and learned that the common-named Malaysian centipede could have killed Eddy and made any of the rest of them extremely sick.

He'd looked at the scorpion books, read the neatly typed labels on each of his son's terrariums before euthanizing them.

Sissy had said Elijah was blind when it came to Gene, gave in to him when he shouldn't.

Sissy had been right.

Words flew to his lips, but he would never say them. Instead, he stroked her smooth hair, rubbed her silky skin.

Please don't leave me. Please never leave.

CHAPTER TWELVE

Children grow up and leave home. The family dog remains till death.
—*Among the God Dogs,* Elijah Workman,
1990

November 3, 1991

"I'M GOING TO EUROPE," said Ezra.

He was calling from Cambridge, Massachusetts. Sissy and Elijah could not have afforded to send Ezra to Harvard, even with the help of scholarships, but Clark and Heloise had pooled resources to let him accept the place he'd won there. And now, in his senior year, he had just announced that he wouldn't be coming home for Christmas, that he was going to Europe instead.

"How are you going to do that?" Sissy asked.

"Clark and Berkeley are helping. And Grandma. And maybe Grandma Workman will, too."

"She doesn't have money to send you to

Europe, Ezra. Why do you have to go at Christmas? Christmas is a family time."

And they had family traditions, Christmas traditions, and they would not be the same without Ezra there. She was infuriated with her mother, with Clark, with anyone who had given him money when she and Elijah hadn't seen him since early June. But she also realized that Ezra was an adult now—twenty-one—and she certainly couldn't stop him going.

She even found herself thinking it was all Elijah's fault for ever insisting that Ezra be told Clark was his natural father. She was forty-seven years old, and abruptly she was miserable and saw the coming Christmas, to which she'd been looking forward, as ruined.

She managed to get off the phone without letting Ezra know her real feelings.

Five minutes later, the phone rang again. She answered with a curt, "Hello?"

"Mom, it's Gene."

Gene had gone to the state university for three years, then dropped out to operate his own business full-time. He lived with Sissy's mother, an arrangement which seemed to suit both. Heloise had a servant to cook for her, and she and Gene played card games every night at exactly eight p.m.

But Gene disliked using the telephone, and

Sissy was immediately concerned. "Is everything all right?"

"It's Grandma. I called 911."

Sissy almost asked if this was one of his jokes.

But she didn't. "I'll be right there. I'll come in the car. You wait for me. Can Grandma talk on the phone?"

"No." He hung up.

ELIJAH DROVE IN just as she was leaving. Eddy was at a friend's house and would be there till later that evening.

Sissy got out of her car and into his and told him what Gene had said. Elijah turned his car in their drive and headed back out the gravel roads toward her mother's house, the house where she'd grown up.

Neither of them spoke.

All Sissy could think was that her mother might be dead. After decades of arguments, after Heloise's turnaround about Elijah, her continued censure of Sissy and Sissy's kennel, and after Sissy had learned to accept that maybe she should be grateful for the mother she had, now this.

The ambulance had beaten them to the house, but there was no sign of hurry.

Gene was nowhere in sight.

Elijah looked about for him, suspected he was

in the kennels, and went with Sissy to speak to the paramedics. But they could see a shrouded form on a stretcher, and both knew the truth.

Two weeks later

"CAN'T YOU ASK HIM to just come home for Christmas this year?" Sissy demanded of Elijah for the fifth time. "Can't you ask it for me?"

She wanted Ezra home at Christmas because it would be the first Christmas she spent without her mother.

"Sissy, he's going to grow up. He'll marry, have his own family. He's not going to keep coming home for Christmas for the rest of his life. Let's give *him* the gift of the freedom to do what he wants."

Elijah felt as though they were having the same argument again, the same one they'd had so many times from back when he'd insisted on telling Clark that Ezra was his biological son.

And it quickly became the same argument.

"You never wanted him here anyhow," Sissy said, "after you found out he was Clark's son."

"That's not true." Elijah couldn't believe she would say such a thing. Eddy was out of town again, at a gymnastics meet, which left the two of them alone in the house. In her will, Sissy's mother had left her house to Gene, incredibly, but—even more incredibly—she had left her kennel to Sissy. So Elijah had spent every evening and weekend since his mother-in-law's death moving her kennels to his and Sissy's property and expanding their own facilities in every way he could to make room for ten more dogs. Too many dogs. Sissy knew they couldn't keep them all, but in a display of regret for her long bickering with her mother, she had renamed her kennel Echo Springs Genesis.

Her mother's fantastic bitch Delilah was gone, but her son Oscar, a handsome black-and-tan, had sired several nice litters, and Sissy looked forward to breeding him to her sable bitch Round-Off; Eddy had been responsible for that litter being named for gymnastics moves.

Gene had shown no dismay at the dogs' departing from his grandmother's house. He'd already mentioned to Elijah that he might put up an additional building. He had long since reestablished his arachnid business and was now thinking of expanding to reptiles.

Elijah had been listening to Sissy cry for days. He felt for her, felt for the pain she was feeling at the loss of her mother, a grief he knew would continue for some time. His own mother was ninety-four, still in possession of her health and her wits, still insisting on tending her own garden in the summer, raking her own leaves in the fall. Cole, the husband of Elijah's sister Maureen, had taken over the shoveling in winter.

Anyhow, now Sissy was truly an orphan, and she wanted her own children around her at Christmas.

"It's not that I mind him going to Europe," she said. "I just mind him going at Christmas."

"Sissy, it's going to happen sometime," he repeated. He was reluctant to interfere. Didn't Sissy realize that clinging to Ezra now, when he wanted to be on his own, would only turn him against her and make him resentful? One's children were on loan from the universe, so to speak.

What was more, Elijah was impatient with her over her suggesting that he didn't want Ezra around. No, more than impatient. It infuriated him.

She said, "I should have walked away from you when I knew I was pregnant with him."

Elijah couldn't believe what he was hearing. Not this sentiment that she should have left him at some point or another—maybe that was true, he sometimes thought. But if she had left him when she was pregnant with Ezra, then Gene and Eddy would not exist.

He reminded her of this rather acidly.

"Of course, I didn't mean that!" she snapped. And burst into tears again. "Just leave me alone." She grabbed her parka from a hook on the wall and stalked out to the kennels.

Elijah watched her retreating back before the door closed behind her, the bright blond hair he knew she had highlighted. He remembered that at some point Heloise Atherton had spent some time in a psychiatric unit. Surely this wouldn't be necessary for Sissy? She was just a little irrational sometimes, and he supposed that one's children leaving home for good could make anyone feel that way.

He thought numbly of the Christmases past, of new bicycles he'd found a way to afford, of the Christmas when Ezra was eighteen when Elijah had found him a used World War II aviator's jacket he'd so wanted. The train set he'd built for both boys (and whose boxcar Gene had loaded with scorpions).

Midnight mass, coming home and each child allowed to open one small present, the rest to wait for Christmas morning when they would learn "if Santa came."

His own eyes started to water, and he followed Sissy out the door, pulling on his own coat as he crossed the snow-dappled lawn.

He could see the light in one of the kennel buildings, and he went inside to find her filling water buckets and crying.

He took Cartwheel's bucket from her, hung it in the dog's kennel run and took Sissy in his arms. "I want him to be here, too, Sissy, but can't you see that we mustn't make him feel guilty for doing what he wants to do? It's not right. He's his own person. He belongs to himself."

Sissy said, "I'm sorry. I'm sorry I said those things."

Sissy rarely told him she was sorry, rarely seemed to have regrets about her own behavior.

"Thank you," Elijah said.

He thought of something he'd wanted to wait until Christmas to tell her. He wasn't sure now was the time. He'd gotten the royalty check a week ago, the check that had so exceeded his expectations for *Children and Dogs: Interaction and Development.* He'd hated the title, primarily because he had no university degree and it sounded pretentious to him under the circumstances. But he had to admit, it did describe the topic. He'd called upon not only his experience with his own children, especially Gene, but also his decades of experience investigating animal abuse cases for the Humane Society.

He reflected that Sissy still intended to attend a dog show the following weekend, reflected on how complex the hunt for an excellent bitch was.

He said, "Can I give you your big Christmas present early?"

Sissy stilled, looked up, her face swollen with tears, her eyes unusually dark blue. "What? All right. I don't care."

She would, he knew. She would care. "My royalties were…larger than expected. You know that really perfect bitch you want to find?"

Sissy clutched his sleeves. She didn't seem happy, nor unhappy, nor doubtful, nor sure. She looked up at him.

He nodded.

Tears leaked from her eyes again. "It's going to be awful without him here. And what about when the others stop coming home?"

Elijah felt certain that one of their children would always come home for Christmas. Gene liked his family well enough and didn't like other people very much at all. But Elijah believed he would always show up on Christmas Day, at least, to be with his family. If not, he'd at least let his parents go to him.

"Let's enjoy the present," he told Sissy. "All right?"

December 24, 1991

TIME, SISSY HAD HOPED, would have taught her not to burst into tears when Ezra called from Boston that night. He was leaving on his flight early the next morning, and was spending Christmas Eve with Clark's parents.

This Christmas, Elijah's mother, Maureen, her husband, Cole, and their five year old, Silas, would be joining her and Elijah and Eddy. Sissy did not care for Cole and knew Elijah didn't, either. Though he helped Elijah's mother with yardwork, he held down no job. Maureen supported them with her job at the bank in downtown Echo Springs.

Also, Cole drank too much, and Sissy had already seen evidence that he was a mean drunk. She dreaded his nastiness being part of their Christmas, especially when she was mourning her mother and the absence of Ezra.

Gene had promised to come for dinner at 6:00 p.m. He had a car now and an unblemished driving record, though Sissy sometimes wondered at this. Still, he liked to drive to the courier offices both to pick up shipments for his business and to drop them off.

At 4:00 p.m., Elijah's sister and brother-in-law and nephew arrived, Maureen carried in the bags of gifts, while Cole allowed Elijah's mother to take his arm.

"They're not smoking in the house," Sissy murmured to Elijah, watching through the backdoor window right before opening it.

"They won't." Elijah bit down a sigh. He had

invited his mother to live with him and Sissy years earlier, but Rosemary Workman wanted to live out her years in her own house. Consequently, Maureen's family—or more precisely, Maureen's husband—made the rules in Rosemary's house. This meant his mother and all her treasured possessions had been exposed to cigarette smoke in the last years of her life. Elijah had told Maureen his feelings about this, and Maureen had said exactly nothing.

Then he had understood that Maureen was afraid of her husband, that his own mother was, as well. And he wasn't sure what to do about it. His mother wanted Maureen and Silas to live with them, and she accepted her daughter's husband as part of that package.

Cole matched his already slightly unsteady steps to Rosemary's as Elijah stepped out. He then moved away from his mother-in-law, saying carelessly, "Now be careful around the dogs, Silas."

Elijah and Sissy exchanged wordless communication, and she followed the five-year-old across the snow. Sissy had never left children, her own or anyone else's, alone with the dogs. Maureen and Cole were, in her loudly and oft spoken opinion, careless with Silas.

Elijah smelled the alcohol coming from Cole as

he passed, and he glanced at Maureen to see what state she was in. His sister didn't drink as much as Cole, but sometimes Elijah thought she drank just to keep Cole company. Her marriage to Cole was her second and somewhat worse than the first.

In her divorce from the first, Maureen had lost custody of her second child, Michelle. Maureen had never recovered from the fact that her ex-husband had been judged a more fit parent. She'd moved back home with her mother and soon after met Cole.

As Elijah helped his mother into the house, he also relieved Maureen of one of her sacks of presents.

"Oh, thanks, Elijah."

He could smell stale cigarette smoke on her skin and in her hair and also all about his mother as he guided her inside, looking down at his hand on her arm, her knuckles swollen with arthritis.

"Hi, Grandma!" Eddy came into the kitchen to hug her.

At twelve, Eddy was compactly built, perfectly proportioned for gymnastics. She wore her blond hair short. Her hair was like Sissy's but her dark eyes and eyelashes were Elijah's. Now she had braces on her teeth, but Elijah could tell she was going to grow into an extremely beautiful woman.

Rosemary Workman put up her face with the small motion of the very elderly, and Eddy kissed her.

Eddy said, "Come and sit down in the living room, Grandma. I'll take you."

Elijah thanked God for this child, who behaved so perfectly, while Cole, rooting through bags at the counter, pulled out a bottle of bourbon and promptly began mixing drinks. "Elijah, anything for you?"

"No, thank you." He wasn't a teetotaler, but he drank seldom, and then only a glass of wine or an occasional beer.

He watched Eddy and his mother make their way to the living room, where his mother exclaimed over the tree.

The house had an open plan, the living room and kitchen adjoined. Now stockings hung by the hearth, Ezra's, too, though he would be on his way to Europe the next day.

Cole, rattling ice in his glass, came into the living room. "Hi, there, Eddy," he said.

"Hello, Uncle Cole," she replied politely. "Where's Silas?"

"Gone to the dogs, I think," he laughed. "In a manner of speaking."

"Mom's with him," Elijah explained to his daughter. Then he thought unexpectedly of the exception to the rule, how even when he was fairly small, Gene had taken to lying down in the kennels.

SILAS WORKMAN STARED at Round-Off through the chainlink fence. "Can he come out?"

"Round-Off is a she," Sissy said, "and I think she'd like to come out. She likes to chase her ball."

Sissy carefully opened the kennel door, releasing only Round-Off and not her sister Spring— Genesis's Handspring. Spring was a bit nippy when excited. Also, Sissy knew Silas was a child who liked to run and yell, and the combination of the two tended to excite dogs.

"Gentle, Round-Off," she told the bitch, who gently put her nose up to Silas's small face and touched him with her pink tongue.

Silas giggled.

"Round-Off, get your ball," Sissy suggested, and Round-Off sprang across the yard, looking about until she found her red rubber ball which she brought back to Sissy. "Do you want to throw it for her?" she asked Silas.

Silas said, "Yes!" and made to snatch the ball.

Sissy did not relinquish it. "Slow down a little, Silas. The dogs aren't so used to children making fast movements around them." Then she handed the ball to her small nephew.

Silas threw it in the way five-year-olds throw, and Round-Off dashed after it, brought it back and sat in front of the boy.

Sissy reflected that if Ezra were here, he would spend his family time with them and then, as soon as he could, rush away to visit high school friends he hadn't seen since his last time home.

Yet here was Silas, whose home life was far less than ideal, who was a small child on Christmas Eve. Not her child, but she could add to his joy on Christmas, and maybe that would help stave off her disappointment at not having Ezra home.

She and Elijah had bought him a Playmobil set for Christmas. Sweaters for Maureen and Rosemary, a coffeemaker for Cole.

Her mother had been coming to their house for Christmas every year for many years now.

Sissy told herself that her mother had lived a full life, that it must be, in very old age, a relief to leave this life, that at least she'd been independent till the end of her days.

When they came inside, Round-Off joined them. Oscar already waited, still depressed at the loss of his mistress. Her mother's dogs had adjusted well to their change of home—at least the dogs with whom they'd always lived came along—but Oscar was a people dog, and he had loved Heloise Atherton. He was the kind of dog who had seemed to take responsibility for his owner. Now he appeared particularly interested in Eddy, but it wasn't until Gene arrived that he really perked up.

Gene said, "Hello, Oscar," in the same uninflected tone in which he said everything. The dog wagged his tail and followed him through the house, and when Gene sat down in the living room, Oscar lay at his feet.

Noticing the change in the dog at Gene's arrival, Sissy wondered if the animal might not be happier with her son. But could she trust Gene to care for such a valuable dog?

Of course, Sissy. He's got a building full of arachnids that he raises with care.

Still, this dog was Sissy's hope to strengthen the lines of her kennel, and she was in no hurry to let him out of her sight.

Cole said, "Can I offer you a whiskey, Gene?"

Gene looked at his uncle without interest. "I don't drink."

"Ah," said Cole. "A chip off the old puritanical block."

Sissy withheld a hiss of annoyance.

Gene said, "The Puritans were Protestants. My father is Catholic."

Unexpectedly, Rosemary erupted in laughter. She reached over and patted her grandson's hand.

Gene jumped up, causing Oscar to leap up, too, and walked out of the house.

Sissy wanted to burst into tears. He would get in the car and drive home now. Damn, damn, damn.

But she didn't hear the car start. Maybe he had gone out to the kennels instead.

"I forgot," Rosemary said, showing her own sharpness in remembering that she'd forgotten her grandson disliked being touched.

Kennedy and Gerry would not be here this Christmas; they were spending the holiday in Kansas City with Gerry's parents. So eventually, the family sat down to dinner. Gene came inside and sat down with them.

Cole said, "Did you get over it?"

Gene behaved as though he wasn't being addressed.

Maureen looked miserable.

Elijah said grace, and they passed dishes, Maureen serving her mother.

"So, how are the bugs?" Cole asked Gene.

Elijah knew his brother-in-law was trying to be friendly, just as he knew that Gene had no special desire to be the center of attention and that he wasn't going to associate the word *bugs* with his business, even to correct Cole.

He would behave as though he hadn't been addressed, which he might believe to be the case, for all Elijah knew.

"I've acquired some Madagascar hissing cockroaches," Gene said pleasantly.

"Can I have one?" said Eddy.

Rosemary shuddered eloquently.

"One," said Sissy. "And nothing venomous."

"What about the spiders and snakes?" Cole asked. "Got any brown recluses?"

"They're a native species without much marketability," Gene replied. "There are undoubtedly some in the crawl space of your house."

"Hey, this kid could work for Orkin!" Cole exclaimed.

Gene did not respond to this.

Dinner passed uneventfully, Ezra called to wish them a merry Christmas. Hearing his voice, Sissy found it surprisingly easy not to cry. She was too concerned about the possibility of the now roundly drunk Cole offending Gene or the rest of them. He'd already told a dirty joke which she wished she hadn't heard.

Eddy had listened, then walked out of the room and into her own bedroom and shut the door, a sign of her good breeding, Sissy thought, and probably also of her desire that Cole would leave their family in peace to enjoy Christmas Eve.

When the time came to leave for Midnight

mass, Cole was too drunk to drive, but believed himself to be fully capable. They had arrived in Elijah's mother's car, and Elijah said, "Sissy, I'll drive these folks, and you and Eddy can ride with Gene."

Cole said, "I'm going to drive to church, just like I drove here."

Silas pointed at Gene's car, with its CB antenna. "Can we ride in that car? It has a CB."

Though Gene disliked the telephone, his old black Buick was outfitted with a CB.

Gene said, "It seats only six. There are eight of us."

Silas appealed to his mother. "Can I ride with him."

Maureen nodded, but Cole nearly snarled, "Silas, get in Grandma's car *now.*"

Gene said, "You're too drunk to drive, Uncle Cole. You'll get a DUI, and then the roads will be safer." He walked away over the snowy drive to his car and opened the passenger door for Silas.

Sissy raced to her son's car. "Backseat, Silas. Ladies get to ride in front."

"But then I can't talk on the CB!"

Eddy climbed in behind the driver's seat.

Seeing Elijah slide behind the wheel of his mother's car, despite Cole's ugly looks, Sissy buckled Silas into the front seat of Gene's car and climbed into the back with her daughter. With a small smile over the way her son had stood up to his uncle, she said, "I'm very proud of you, Gene."

Gene said, "Thank you, Mother." In his methodical way, he looked about the car to make sure all his passengers were wearing their seat belts, then he started the car and turned on the headlights.

CHAPTER THIRTEEN

When my uncle Silas died, I took his dogs. Billy Bob, a five-year-old brindle, did not accept my ownership. He found elaborate ways to escape, and he'd return to Uncle Silas's place. I would find Billy Bob there, lying on the back porch, waiting for his master to return.

—*Among the God Dogs,* Elijah Workman, 1990

February 2, 1992

SISSY WAS GLAD when Christmas was over and the new year came. Soon, Round-Off came into heat, and Sissy bred her to Oscar. Then she asked Gene if he would like Oscar to live with him.

Gene had come over for dinner, and Sissy asked him afterward, when they were sitting in the living room together, preparing to play cards, as he had with her mother for so many years. Gene particularly liked gin rummy, but sometimes they played poker instead, though never for money.

He said, "You've never given me a dog, Mother."

"Well, I wasn't planning to *give* you Oscar. I just wanted to know if you'd like him to live with you. I'd continue to buy his food and pay his vet bills."

Gene looked at the dog, who lay beside him as though there was nowhere he'd rather be. "Thank you. I'd like that. Is this because I told Uncle Cole he was too drunk to drive?"

"No," said Sissy. "I just think you're a responsible person."

Eddy came in the back door while the others were playing cards. She'd been babysitting Allie Morgan's niece, Samantha.

Eddy said, "Samantha knows all her ABCs! She did it for her mom when they got home."

"Did you teach her that?" asked Sissy, impressed with her daughter's maturity and sense of responsibility.

"I *helped*. Her parents have been working with her, too, but this is the first time she's gotten them all."

Sissy remembered when she'd confessed to Allie that she was thinking of leaving Elijah—and she remembered Allie's reaction. These days, Sissy never thought of leaving. She thought she wouldn't be able to cope if something happened to Elijah.

He had become the Humane Society's leading investigator of dogfighting rings. Several times he had been asked to divorce himself from Genesis Kennels. It had been called a conflict of interest. He had refused, arguing his case, and no one at the Humane Society wanted to lose him. Now he was in a position where he could quit; the royalties from his books provided enough of an income.

Sissy wanted him to quit, not because she disliked the Humane Society or because many people in the Humane Society were so thoroughly against the breeding of purebred dogs or keeping animals as pets. She wanted Elijah to quit because the work had become increasingly dangerous.

Dogfights were staged by the criminal under-world. Usually dogfighting went hand in hand with drugs, prostitution, guns, violence. The stakes and the risks were high.

He was on the road in all kinds of weather, some-times driving hundreds of miles to matches. He did not speak of what he saw at home, but Sissy had been woken more than once by his disturbed sleep.

Sissy knew he'd be gone all night tonight. He never told her precisely where he was going when he was working. He would say no more than "south" or something even less specific. He would call her from the road when it was all over to tell her he was safe. Sissy understood that he believed that if his cover was blown these people could come for his family or something like that. What he did was a mystery to her, unlike that first dogfight they'd attended decades before, when the laws were weaker, when those involved could expect no more than a slap on the hand.

Now what troubled him, he said, was that the people matching dogs were so often kids, teenagers.

"Why don't they train dogs in Obedience?" Sissy had asked.

"They're trying to make money, Sissy."

She knew how little financial profit there was in obedience training.

"You won't ever let him off-lead?" Sissy pressed suddenly to Gene. "I mean, outside Grandma's yard or the house. When you're *out.*"

Gene thought this over. "All right. He comes when he's called, you know."

"Yes, but still."

"All right," he repeated.

Eddy joined them in the living room.

"Oscar's going to live with Gene," Sissy told her daughter.

Eddy looked interested. "Mom, can I have a snake?"

To go with her hissing cockroach.

"Aren't snakes more high-maintenance than cockroaches?" asked Sissy. Though a copperhead had once bitten Ezra, Sissy was not revolted by snakes in the way she was by scorpions.

Gene said, "Corn snakes are native. They don't require the same level of attention to humidity that ball pythons do, for instance."

"How big do they get?" Sissy asked. "And what do they eat?"

"Frozen-thawed mice," Gene said. "That should be no problem with a corn snake. Sometimes ball pythons are a bit picky. Eddy could have one from one of the clutches this summer. They get about four feet long, Mother."

"If you can wait till this summer," Sissy told Eddy, "and if it's all right with your father, then the answer is yes."

That same night

THE STAGED FIGHTS were in Des Moines. Elijah showed up with Keller—a recent pit bull rescue renamed from Killer—and a shifty look. He'd heard of the fights, he said, from a guy downtown.

This group of dog owners was unusually youthful, predominantly black and mixed race, and Elijah felt out of place. He'd barely learned to navigate safely among gangs, and he knew there were gang members here. He had a bad feeling and knew enough to pay attention to it.

But he was already in, at the abandoned house on the outskirts of town. There were young girls, too, and an older black man who looked to Elijah like a pimp.

Elijah knew abruptly that he needed to walk away from this. He stuck out like a sore thumb, he was afraid, and he knew that other people could smell and feel fear. He made his way back to the entrance.

The doorman looked at him but didn't object when Elijah walked out.

Across the street, the door of a burgundy sedan slammed, and an attractive black woman in high heels, dressed in a black pantsuit that a business-woman might wear, strode across the street.

Elijah was arrested by the sight of her. She was beautiful, and she didn't fit in here. She headed into the house, and he heard her shouting at someone, and then one of the gang members was pushing her outside.

She yelled, "Jackson Trimball, you get out here right now!"

The doorman blocked her from going back inside the building. He made a vaguely apolo-getic gesture, smooth and urbane.

Elijah was still in sight of the building. He

couldn't do anything but keep going, get to his own vehicle, a ten-year-old Toyota 4-Runner, parked several blocks away. He couldn't go to the rescue of this woman, if she needed it.

He hurried without looking as though he was hurrying, feeling like a coward when it wasn't cowardice but duty to his job that had kept him from exposing himself.

He glanced back and saw the woman lunge at the doorman.

His instincts continued to tell him to leave.

Then the woman was down, and there were three tall young men staring at her, their message plain. She needed to leave.

Elijah kept walking with Keller, hating himself.

At his truck, he put Keller in the back, looked in his rearview mirror and finally saw headlights coming up the street. The burgundy car.

The woman was holding something to her face, a piece of fabric.

Let it go, Elijah.

Another car followed her, and Elijah recognized it because it had been parked outside the abandoned house. The dogfighters were going to make sure she left. Maybe make sure of other things, too.

Elijah pulled out his cell and punched the code for his partner with the Des Moines police, who was supposed to raid the fight. He briefly related what had happened, then gave the license numbers of the two cars he was following. "Can you check on this lady?" he asked. "Make sure she's okay."

"This isn't going according to plan," the policeman replied. "Did they make you?"

"I don't know. Maybe."

"We're going to raid. Can't do anything about this lady. Wouldn't worry about it."

Easy for him to say.

Elijah followed the two cars along the highway, but eventually the car with the gang members in it turned off the road, no doubt heading back to the fights.

The woman was going to be okay. She'd make it home.

Her son was in a gang and matching dogs, that had to be what she'd been doing there, and Elijah wanted to help her.

But he had no pretext for doing so.

He headed south.

SISSY STARTED out of her sleep. Elijah. He was there in the bedroom, home in the middle of the night.

"You're back," she said.

"I'm resigning," he said. He couldn't tell her all

the whys. That the house had been full of kids, kids younger than his sons, even some boys who looked Eddy's age, wasn't the whole answer.

That he hadn't gone to the aid of a woman in distress wasn't the whole answer, either.

It had to do with something else, that he'd felt a dangerous curiosity and attraction toward the woman, that he'd wanted to follow her all the way home, to ask her what she'd been doing there, to offer to help her with her son. Which was all so much romantic fantasy.

And it wasn't the first time he'd found other women attractive since he'd been married to Sissy, nor the first time he'd thought of trying to meet one. What bothered him was that this time he'd actually been afraid he would go through with it and afraid of the reason behind it.

For the first time, he'd begun to find his world with Sissy narrow and had really considered venturing outside its confines. And he'd begun to rationalize why he was doing so.

He hadn't, of course, and he didn't know the name of the woman he'd seen at the house. He'd been impressed by her fierce determination to get her son out of there.

And some small place inside him had remembered that Sissy had deceived him about Ezra's parentage.

As though that might excuse his straying.

He didn't want to stray, to be the kind of person who strayed, and so he would remove himself from temptation and focus on writing and the kennels and being close to Sissy.

"What will you do?" Sissy asked.

"Something," he said. "Maybe something positive."

Sissy said, "You're not going to be unemployed, are you?"

Elijah was undressing, and he glanced toward the bed. "No, Sissy. I'm not planning to stop working." Ironic, he thought, that it was a step he was taking for her, and now she was reacting badly to it, when she'd so many times said she wished he would find something else. "I put Keller in the end kennel, the Pre-fert."

"Who is Keller?"

"Pit bull, rescued last week in Jefferson City. She's nice."

"To people," Sissy remarked. "We can't have her here." She would attack one of their dogs, the show dogs, and do real damage.

"I know," Elijah said tiredly. "But I didn't want to take her back to the pound before I came home tonight."

"I hope she can't get out," Sissy said.

Elijah looked into the future with a feeling of

depression and dread. A future of Sissy and her Westminster dreams.

She said, "I let Gene take Oscar home."

This surprised Elijah and touched him. He'd noticed Sissy's increasing appreciation for Gene since her mother's death. "Was he pleased?"

"Oh, you know Gene. I think so."

Elijah laughed softly and climbed into bed, reaching for her, for her familiar shape and her familiar scent and accepting her familiar values, her unchanging selfishness.

"And Eddy wants a snake."

Elijah gave a small shudder. He didn't care for them.

"I'll protect you," Sissy told him.

July 3, 1992

GENE HAD INVITED his parents to come over to his house, Sissy's childhood home, on their anniversary. He wanted, he said, to surprise them.

Sissy had never known their anniversary to occur under so much strain. Since quitting work for the Humane Society, Elijah had been writing more than ever and was trying his hand at fiction—science-fiction, no less, featuring a Humane Society investigator in a future age. His agent was excited about the premise.

Unfortunately, however, Elijah was also looking into starting a nonprofit. He'd told Sissy, "Sometimes the problem with taking the animals out of the home is that the people causing the problems will start on the kids." He believed that right treatment of people could be developed from first learning gentleness with animals, and he wanted to set up some kind of camp for disadvantaged kids where they would care for animals.

Sissy hated the idea. As far as she was concerned it would mean that Elijah would make less money than he could writing full-time—he *was* successful—and that he'd be less involved with their *joint* business of Echo Springs Genesis German Shepherd Dogs.

He responded to her complaints predictably—with cool aloofness. In fact, he'd shown her so little warmth lately that she wondered if he would give her an anniversary gift this year. He hadn't mentioned it so far.

She had bought something for him—a new laptop computer—*hint, hint, Elijah, be a writer, don't start your nonprofit.* He'd seemed a little dismayed. Though he made more money writing than working for the Humane Society, he still thought of himself as being out of work.

Ezra, who was now an attorney in Chicago, said

on the phone, "It's his work ethic, Mom. That's how Dad is."

It distressed Sissy that Ezra chose to live so far from Echo Springs, but he insisted that he liked being in "the city." There was no city in Missouri that he considered comparable to Chicago. Sissy couldn't help wondering if Ezra stayed so far away because he felt less a part of their family than Gene did.

"I wonder how Gene is going to surprise us," Sissy said for the third time as they drove to the house where she'd grown up, the house that had been her mother's.

"Maybe with a pet snake," Elijah said uneasily.

"I don't think they've hatched yet. Well, the ball pythons hatch. I'm not sure if the corn snakes are born from eggs or born live. He keeps talking about monitor lizards, too. Do you know what they are?"

"I know that the Komodo dragon is the world's largest."

"He can't breed those, can he?" asked Sissy.

Elijah shook his head. "Most of Monitors aren't so big, but none of them have what you'd call gentle dispositions. We used to get them into the Humane Society occasionally."

Gene was nowhere in sight when they parked. They got out of the car, glancing about and heard Oscar's baritone bark from inside combined with another sound, another bark, not so deep.

Sissy and Elijah exchanged glances as they climbed the steps to the porch and knocked.

Gene opened the door almost immediately. He had a leash in his hand, and on the end of the leash was a sable German shepherd puppy. A female, ears up.

The puppy was wearing a pink ribbon.

Sissy blinked, wondering by what stretch of the imagination Gene thought they needed another puppy and believed that he was the proper person to pick one out.

He said, "Her kennel name is Starry Night Marie Curie."

Sissy's eyes widened. The Starry Night Kennel was in Canada, and their dogs were good. The owners maintained that they had kept their lines free of megaesophagus, a genetic condition that had begun to plague Sissy's. A dog with an enlarged esophagus regurgitated food and was at increased risk of aspirating. Such a dog couldn't even be sold as a pet, but must be given for free to someone willing to assume the risks and trouble of having such an animal.

The puppy was pretty, too, Sissy had to admit. "How on earth— Why did you do this, Gene?"

"You like dogs, and I could afford it," he said

proudly. "I decided if you don't have room for her she can live here with me and Oscar."

"I think we can find room for her," Elijah said, biting down a smile. He knew full well that Sissy was probably hating the fact that she hadn't been able to choose the puppy, but this one had a very pretty face. "It's a generous gift, Gene."

"Well, it was actually a trade. I had a clown ball python, and they were interested in her."

Elijah did not marvel that the snake and the dog were of equal value. He knew the prices placed on exotic reptiles.

They stepped into the foyer, and Sissy crouched down to pet the puppy, then glanced up and seemed to notice something for the first time.

"Gene Workman, what have you done to your grandmother's house?"

Gene behaved as though he heard no censure in her tone. "It's part of my surprise for you. You were worried about how Oscar's getting along. I did it for him."

Gene had, throughout the house, cut waist-high doors in various walls and plastered the edges of the openings. "I don't like to leave doors open," he explained, "so this way I don't have to get up when Oscar wants to go somewhere else. It makes it easier for him to patrol."

"But now you have all these open dog-sized doors," Sissy reasoned.

"It's not the same," Gene replied placidly.

Oscar gave a big dog smile and raced back and forth through two doors, which gave him a nice long indoor running stretch. Marie Curie sat down and watched him.

When they returned home that night, Sissy entered the bedroom to find a white hooded sweatshirt, with a picture of a German shepherd on the front lying on her pillow. Not at any dog show had she seen either such a nice representation of the breed or such a nice all-cotton sweatshirt.

She picked it up and looked at Elijah, then pulled it on.

Only then did she discover the envelope in the front pocket. Elijah watched as she drew out tickets to the Chicago ballet.

"That's just one thing I thought we'd do," he said. "Ezra's taking four days off to spend with us."

Sissy turned to him, trying to forget her bad feelings, especially the one that somehow he had chased Ezra away—first by insisting that Ezra know Clark and the reverse, then in not joining her to beg Ezra to stay near home.

She said, "Thank you, Elijah."

He smiled, but she felt again the distance between them. *He's just going through the motions,* she thought. *There's no romance left for him.* But she didn't know what to do about it. Some days she felt the same way.

June 3, 1993

SISSY WISHED, not for the first time in the past year and a half, that Elijah had never quit working as an investigator for the Humane Society. She'd even found herself saying, "Why couldn't you just devote yourself to the kennels?"

But Elijah couldn't. Elijah had started the nonprofit Bless the Beasts, a camp for inner-city kids who had been in trouble that taught them to care for animals and treat them with gentleness, reasoning that people who are kind to animals will refrain from being violent toward people.

The camp property was a long parcel down the road from their home. The animals included cats, dogs, rabbits, nonvenomous reptiles, birds and horses. Elijah was its director and had hired three counselors, all college-age. A local veterinarian volunteered three hours a week to see to the animals and to give the kids talks on veterinary medicine.

The vet was an attractive woman named Corinne Foster. She was thirty-eight years old, divorced from a violent man, and Elijah seemed especially interested in hearing about that situation, as Maureen was still married to Cole.

On Eddy's last day of eighth grade, a half day, Sissy spent the afternoon with her daughter in Kansas City, driving Gene's half-ton pickup truck—his business's main vehicle—and picking up agility equipment for her training business and some home gymnastics equipment she'd promised Eddy if she got straight A's. Elijah had been against all the purchases, saying that they shouldn't spoil Eddy and that the dog-training business should pay for itself—which it didn't when you tallied up agility equipment.

So Sissy was surprised by the willingness with which Elijah unloaded their purchases when they got home.

Soon he was talking about Corinne. "She says she didn't leave her husband until it passed the threshold of what she'd been used to growing up. But my father wasn't an alcoholic. He wasn't mean to my mother or any of us. So why does Maureen stay with Cole?"

It was unanswerable. Sissy moved the agility equipment to where she wanted it in the yard, repositioning a tunnel. It was 8:00 p.m. but still not dark. She watched a firefly blink nearby, then looked at Elijah. "Are you attracted to her?"

She saw it in the dusk. He flushed.

"She *is* attractive," he said, an evasive answer if Sissy had ever heard one.

"Are you involved with her?" Sissy demanded. She wasn't sure she'd know if Elijah ever became involved with another woman. He was aloof toward her most of the time; how would she recognize a change?

"Of course not. She volunteers at the camp. I'm married. I would never be unfaithful to you."

Sissy believed him. She also believed that he might *wish* to be unfaithful but not do so, that he was capable of carrying a torch for another woman without any declaration of love, any physical manifestation. Well, how far could that go?

She tried to quiet her doubts. But she could see that Elijah was smitten with this other woman, that he admired her. Corinne had a twelve-year-old son, and Elijah had remarked what a good mother she was.

Now he added, "She's not like that, either, Sissy. She's like us. Her husband was her childhood sweetheart. She's never been with another man."

Sissy had reached for a long-handled scoop to clean up after one of the dogs, a spot she'd just seen, but she stopped, stared at him.

Elijah glanced at her, then turned his attention to setting up one of the agility jumps.

"In just what context did she vouchsafe *that* confession?" Sissy asked. "What were you talking about that made her feel comfortable telling you how many lovers she's had?"

Elijah heard the question and tried to convince himself that Sissy's tone was unwarranted. Corinne Foster had found his to be a sympathetic ear for her small frustrations in being a single parent, her discomfort around most men, her fear of dating. He'd thought of himself as a sort of older brother to her. But now he wondered, *It's more than that, isn't it, Elijah?*

Corinne seemed to have a sort of hero-worship for him, speaking admiringly of the kind of husband and father he was, of the compassion required to be director of Bless the Beasts.

He was going to have to stop it, stop listening to her confidences, discourage her from confiding. Sissy was right.

He wanted to walk over to his wife, to reassure her of his love, but right now he felt as guilty as if he *had* been unfaithful.

Sissy let three of the dogs into the yard, including her favorite of Round-Off's puppies, a promising black-and-tan bitch named Coco. She tossed a ball for Round-Off, then murmured, only loudly enough for Elijah to hear, "I guess you think she's more pure than I am because you weren't my first."

Elijah's breath caught. Not in shock that she could say something like this after twenty-plus years of marriage to him. No.

Because some small part of him did feel this way.

Pure wasn't the word.

Sissy was passionate, more passionate than good. He'd always loved her in spite of this, but he still admired old-fashioned values.

Something he'd vowed never to ask came out of his mouth. "Was Clark?"

Sissy felt hot anger surge through her. How dare he care about this? She walked up to him in the growing darkness. "No. But I've been faithful to you since I walked away from Clark, and I don't deserve your censure on this. Especially not from someone who seems to be playing a little loose with his own vows."

"That's not true."

But she had already stalked past him and into the house.

He felt small for having criticized her and knew that his questions really came from the pain, so many years ago, of learning that Ezra was not his biological son.

CHAPTER FOURTEEN

Men had been matching dogs for centuries, but never before had animal abuse investigators had to deal with the effects of something like ArgRan. Worse, the dogs' brains had been surgically altered so that they would not stop fighting even to save themselves. D'Angeles hated breaking up fighting rings because the dogs couldn't be kept as pets, not unless it could be arranged that they would never see another dog.

—*Gone to the Dogs: A Nick D'Angeles Mystery,* Elijah Workman, 1993

June 10, 1994

EDDY LIKED HELPING her father at Bless the Beasts, and he paid her decently, too. She worked in the office, organizing the paperwork on the campers. She helped with the grounds, planting flowers around the office building. Most of the time, the campers—or clients as they were sometimes called—cared for the animals, but sometimes Eddy gave them pointers on teaching obedience to the dogs.

Her father had just gotten off the phone to a grant-writer and was getting ready to make his next call. Eddy had been collating orientation sheets for the first summer session, which would begin the following week.

She'd been thinking of something for a while, had even mentioned it to Ezra on the phone, though her oldest brother, she had to admit, hadn't been keen. Gene, strangely, had been more interested. "Dad, do you and Mom have any special romantic traditions? Well, like, I know about the dog presents on your anniversary." She hadn't meant to say that word, then decided the slip didn't hurt at all. "Do you have a song or anything?"

Her father had been turning a page in the steno pad he used to write down things he needed to do that day. He stilled or seemed to. He didn't look at Eddy. "Yes."

Eddy waited for him to say more.

"The first song we danced to." He seemed especially economical with his words. "It's called 'Let It Be Me.'"

"I've never heard of it."

"Not surprised." He turned his steno page. "How does it go?"

Everything in Elijah had filled with pain. He could remember the last time he'd heard the song. Fourth of July, several years before. He'd been refinishing the deck, and Sissy had done some of the sanding, still looking amazing in shorts and a bikini top, and she'd had on some radio station that was playing golden oldies, greatest hits of whatever year. It had come on.

She'd looked over at him, seeming half-frightened.

He hadn't been able to do anything because he'd remembered the time he'd heard it before that—leaving the hospital after Ezra's snakebite.

He wished he could summon the romantic feelings, the intensely passionate feelings, that he used to have for Sissy. But something in him had changed. He was grateful for his life, grateful for his children and his work, grateful for his beautiful wife. But things were different.

He had become very attracted to a divorced veterinarian. After Sissy had said what she had to him about it, he'd become aloof toward Corrine. Then, when she'd tried to share another personal confidence, he'd said, "I really can't listen to this. I'm attracted to you, Corinne, but I'm married, and I'm going to stay married."

She had asked if he would prefer she not help out at Bless the Beasts.

He'd told her that he had no way of replacing what she did.

So she had continued to come, but she was obviously saddened by the distance between them, and he'd had to curb his feelings constantly until he felt like begging her to never return. Then, this spring, she'd moved away, and now a young male veterinarian came to see the animals and talk to the kids.

But things were not the same with Sissy, and now Eddy had asked him about that song.

Well, he felt nothing, so why not. He tried to remember, and he sang a few lines for his daughter.

She said, "I've heard that song! That's so romantic, Dad."

He stood up, saying, "I've got to check on Mr. Rogers." One of the birds, named by a camper. He had no reason to check on the bird, who'd had surgery recently but was fine. Elijah just had to get out of the office, get away from his daughter's eyes, because his own were betraying him.

He strode through the damp heat toward the aviary, and once inside, he leaned against a pole and tried to compose himself, tried to rearrange his whole being into someone he used to be.

EDDY RODE HER RACING BIKE to her brother's house. Oscar appeared in the doorway of the Quonset hut where Gene kept his breeding animals, and Eddy headed over to the building, got off and leaned her bike against it.

He was inside, feeding crickets to the tarantulas and scorpions.

"I found out they had a song," she said without preamble. "'Let It Be Me' by the Everly Brothers. So if we can get a band, we can get them to play it. Can we have a band, Gene?" For their parents' surprise twenty-fifth wedding anniversary celebration.

"I don't like bands," Gene said. "I don't think Mom and Dad do, either."

"It won't be a party without a band. Don't go all Ezra on me and say you're not sure it's a great idea."

"Is that what Ezra said?"

"He pointed out that they eloped after Mom left someone else—'my father, by the way' was how he put it—at the altar. I said, 'So what?'"

Gene said, "We should definitely have a big celebration."

"I told him you thought so, and he said, 'That figures.'"

Gene gave the ghost of a smile, which was as close as Gene ever came to smiling.

"He also said that I think everything's all hearts and flowers between Mom and Dad, but it's not."

Gene looked at her, then opened another tarantula "shoebox" and dropped in crickets, made a notation on the container's pad of paper and moved to the next.

"Is that true?" Eddy suddenly demanded.

"Is what true?"

"That there's something wrong between them."

Gene gave another of his small half smiles.

"Is it true?" Eddy demanded again.

"I don't know," Gene answered.

"But you think we should have an anniversary party?"

"Yes," he said.

She finally took off her bike helmet and resumed planning. "So, it will be Fourth of July weekend…"

June 30, 1994

SISSY WATCHED Elijah climb into bed. They'd both slept naked throughout most of their marriage. It amazed Sissy how good he still looked at fifty, his stomach hard, his shoulders and arms muscular. Granted, he'd never been work shy, and she knew he did carpentry around the camp as he did home. He kept his hair short, and it had gone iron-gray over the years, but with his dark complexion and rugged features he seemed even more attractive than he had been when he was younger.

As she slid into bed beside him, she wondered if he would reach for her this night.

He did. He turned to her with a characteristic sweetness that retained its remoteness and said, "And how is my wife?"

I'm still his wife, she thought. And he did tell her that he loved her. But she never knew what was going on inside of him. Never in their whole married life could she remember him discussing his emotions.

As he touched her, touched her intimately, she whispered, "I wish you were still in love with me."

He stilled, his hand cupping her gently. Elijah had no idea how to answer. "What makes you think I'm not, Sissy?"

His answer brought a lump to her throat. Why hadn't he just denied it, said he loved her as much as ever?

"Never mind. I think I sometimes expect too much of you."

Elijah wondered if this was true. "I love you," he said. "My God, Sissy. You're the only woman I've ever been…close to. You're my wife, the mother of my children." He felt the emotion in his throat that he'd known when Eddy had asked him about the romance in her parents' marriage. He put his lips against her hair, which smelled like her apple-scented shampoo.

Sissy wanted romance and passion from him. He held her closer. "I love you," he repeated.

"I don't know what I've done to make you… disenchanted with me."

He *was* disenchanted in some way, but it didn't matter, did it?

Just to her because somehow he'd let it show. "I'm disenchanted with myself, if anyone. It's nothing to do with you." As he spoke, he realized this was the truth. He'd been idealistic when he was younger, even when he was still working for the Humane Society. Now he knew he was helping kids get away from dogfighting and other types of animal abuse, helping them to become better people. But somehow he'd pictured himself and Sissy doing something together. Not just the kennel. Something to improve the world. Their children were almost all grown. Wasn't it time?

He kissed the top of Sissy's head, then lifted her face, drew her lips toward his, touching her beautiful, healthy body, still muscled from playing tennis.

She said, "I'm going to be on the radio next week. Talking about dog training."

"Local radio?"

"The public radio station." She paused. "They asked if you might join me."

"Really." It wasn't a question. Just a thought. *How can I grow back with her,* he thought, *if we don't work together on what matters to us?*

And they did both care about dogs, though they expressed it in different ways. "How do you feel about that?" he asked.

"I think it might be fun."

"I'll do it," he agreed.

Sissy felt his caressing of her resume and wished she hadn't revealed her anxiety about the depth of his love for her. She kissed him back, becoming for a time the wild girl who'd been in love with him so long ago, who'd seduced him the same day she'd left Clark at the altar.

July 3, 1994

SISSY WAS ECSTATIC. Marie would be going to the Eukanuba show. *Westminster, Westminster,* she thought. Marie wasn't a bitch of her breeding of course, but the Starry Night bitch Gene had gotten for her.

She was going to breed Oscar and Marie after the show.

Elijah said they had too many dogs now, and he was right, Sissy knew. They had two sixth-month-old pet dogs from Leia's last litter, and a year-old boy with megaesophagus from Round-Off's.

Sissy couldn't tell which side the mega had come from and wondered if she should breed Round-Off again. Of course, there'd been no mega in the previous litter....

The sound of Jet Skis from the lake was incessant. It was Sunday, and Sissy told herself, *Two more days*. Two more days and the riotous Fourth of July weekend would be over.

She'd hoped Ezra would come down from Chicago, but he'd said he was spending the weekend with his girlfriend's family. Sissy knew that today was her twenty-fifty wedding anniversary, but she couldn't work up any excitement about the fact. Certainly many marriages didn't last that long, and hers wasn't a bad marriage. Yet the dreams of her girlhood which should have come true, which she'd believed were coming true in her marriage to Elijah, had somehow gone awry.

Not that there weren't those occasional times when she felt especially close to him while making love, or when she especially appreciated something funny he said, something that was so Elijah. And only Elijah could really appreciate the funniness of Gene cutting waist-high doors in the walls of her mother's house, now dubbed by Eddy "the Hole in the Wall." Sissy hadn't thought it was funny at first, of course.

She was still deeply attracted to Elijah, but it was too tiring to try to make him love her back. The time when she'd feared he might begin an affair with another woman—even leave her for another woman—was gone, and had been even before the beautiful veterinarian moved away.

The problem was that she wanted him to love her—to nearly worship her as he had long ago. Now he seemed resigned to her faults and failings. What was more, she no longer had the confidence that came from being a little bit wild. In the years since she'd stopped teaching drama at the high school, her life had become increasingly tame, and she felt this as cowardice on her part. Especially since she knew Elijah didn't share her strong desire to get to Westminster.

"Well, we're going to get there anyway, aren't we, Marie?" she told the pretty bitch.

"Get where?"

It was Elijah. He'd come out into the morning sunlight on the lawn, barefoot and dressed in swim trunks and nothing else.

"Westminster," Sissy answered matter-of-factly.

"Yes, I think you are."

You? If only he had said *we.*

"Eddy's up to something with Gene," he said.

Sissy glanced up. "Like what?"

"I have a feeling we're in for a surprise party."

"What?" She was dressed in her kennel-cleaning clothes and had thought of putting off washing her hair for another day.

"Just a guess," he said. "But someone did call and ask if this was where we wanted the keg delivered."

"Keg! Gene doesn't even drink, and Eddy's not of age!"

"It occurred to me it was somebody's idea of a joke. But then they wanted to know if this was the address of the party. So I think we should just act surprised."

And wash my hair, Sissy thought.

"It is our twenty-fifth," he said. He'd already wished her a happy anniversary when he awoke beside her that morning.

He'd thought long what to get her for this milestone. By the night last week when she'd asked again if he was still in love with her—or more precisely said that she wished he was—he still hadn't chosen a present. She'd told him then what she wanted.

She wanted him to be in love with her, to feel his passion.

But for him, that would mean facing again the moment of learning she'd lied to him about Ezra, the hurt of that moment. He needed to somehow transcend that pain. On top of that, he must somehow undo the damage he'd done to her, by valuing her less than he should have.

So he'd made his own plan for this day.

"Want to go out in the canoe?"

She looked at him in surprise. "I've got to shower and wash my hair before this party."

"Your hair is beautiful and smells good," he said, catching her hand. "Come out in the canoe with me."

"And there are all those people on Jet Skis."

"I know where we can get away from them."

"Should we take any of the dogs?"

He thought about this. "One well-behaved dog."

"We'll take Marie, then. She needs a bath anyhow. I was going to do that today."

"We'll let her be a dog today," Elijah said.

HE TOOK HER around the corner to Eugene Cove, not named for their son. It was the cove where the camp lay, and this weekend there were no campers. The shoreline was deserted when he pulled up the canoe.

Marie jumped out and raced about, sniffing. Sissy had brought her lead, and now she called to her and put it on the bitch.

Elijah took her hand and led her up to one of

the open cabins, four walls that reached only to waist-level, screens going up the rest of the way.

He'd made the place ready, with flowers on one window ledge and sheets and a quilt on one of the beds and a cassette player that was going to make him face the music.

Inside the cabin, they let Marie off her lead again, and Elijah found, at the base of the flowers, his gift for Sissy. It was a small soapstone dog, but she couldn't know that because it was wrapped in a piece of paper.

Sissy took it, unwrapped it, and found that the paper was shaped in a heart. She wanted words, but there were none on it.

Elijah switched on the boombox. "Will you dance with me?"

She did, going into his arms as he played the song that had once been *their* song, back when they had been in love, before she'd lied about Ezra, before he'd learned the truth.

Holding her, Elijah listened to the words, remembering when he'd felt like begging her to cling to him, only to him.

And she had done that.

He didn't want her to see his face, and he wasn't dancing, just holding her. He sang the words softly to her, his voice not his own. He knew he was trembling and hated the fact, just as he hated the memory of the aloneness of learning his oldest son was not his.

His eyes burned, and he fought the tears. Was he going to have to walk out and get himself back together?

Sissy squirmed loose, not free but so that she could look up at him.

His dark lashes were wet.

"Oh, God," she said. "Elijah."

"I'm fine." He blinked, making it go away, resisting the need to flee. He stayed and kept himself together, and she touched his face, touched his eyebrows and beneath his eyes.

She said, "What's wrong? Please."

"Nothing's wrong. Everything's as right as it can be." The song started again. It would play three times, the way she'd played it on their wedding day.

He drew her toward the bed, knowing he couldn't go as far as she wanted, couldn't say all the things she wanted to hear. Because what would come out was childish. *It hurts. It hurt then, and it still hurts, and it will always hurt.*

He'd believed she was just his. Now she had been for twenty-five years, and he was sick about something she really hadn't been able to help.

"Is this still about Ezra?" she asked.

He closed his eyes, his breath shaking. "I love you," he said. "Everything's fine."

"Please tell me. You've never…" Sissy didn't know quite what to say, nor how to say it.

"Never what?"

They sat down on the bed, then lay down.

"You've never said how you felt. When you learned… about Ezra."

He couldn't help it. There was nothing else to say. "How do you think I felt?"

Sissy made herself look into his dark eyes. "Did you think I was a virgin?"

"I didn't *want* to think about it. It's not just that. I didn't dream you'd slept with Clark, though. I don't know why."

"He wasn't the first. When I was in school, I fell in love with a professor. We were lovers. Then I found out he was married, so that was that. It hurt." Sissy had never told him this, and she felt knots in her chest untying as she spoke. "And Clark— Elijah, it's as I told you. I wasn't sure I wanted to marry him, and I decided to…be with him to convince myself. And it had the opposite effect. It's probably why I left him at the altar. It was once, Elijah, and Ezra came from that, and I will never apologize for wanting my son or wanting him to be exactly who he is."

"I would never ask you to apologize for that. God, I always wanted Ezra, Sissy. It never made me not want Ezra."

"Just me."

"It didn't make me not want you."

"Then what?" Sissy asked, frustrated. "What?"

He could not say the words. Was she so emotionally disabled that she had to hear them, that she couldn't figure it out for herself. He said very softly, "I was hurt. I went out to the car and when I started it the radio came on, and it was this song, Sissy. And this song, corny nineteen-sixty vintage, expressed how I had always felt about you, how much I loved you."

Sissy heard the melody and lyrics in the background as he spoke, and she suddenly clung to him desperately, holding his head. "Elijah, I never wanted to hurt you. God, that's why I was going to take that secret to the grave! I never wanted you to know."

His head against her throat, he heard her. She had planned to keep Ezra's parentage secret always. Not out of deceit, but to protect him from the pain Elijah had felt when he discovered the truth. Because she'd known how much it would hurt.

He hugged her, and suddenly a pink tongue slurped across his face beside a snuffling oversized black nose. "Hey, Marie," he said, letting the dog kiss both him and Sissy.

He looked at Sissy and said, "I never knew that."

She kissed him, and he held her closer, now allowing the tears he hadn't let come out before, because these few tears were not bitter but comfortable, as comfortable as his wife of twenty-five years.

Marie did not give up, and Sissy said, "Okay, Marie. Go lie down. Elijah and I are having quality time."

The bitch, looking chastened, moved away, turned in circles and lay down on the floor.

Then Sissy kissed Elijah's eyes. She lay on top of him.

He said, "I wonder when we have to be back for that damned party. They're going to play this song. Eddy was quizzing me about it."

Sissy said, "I can never hear it too many times, Elijah. I love you the way I did when I was sixteen, when I was twelve, and all the ways I've loved you since." She giggled. "They got a keg. I can't believe it. And Gene hates parties."

Elijah played with the buttons on her blouse, beginning to undo them.

Sissy asked, "Are we okay again? Like I've wanted to be all my married life?"

He closed his eyes and whispered an oath, and she didn't know what it meant. He just said again, "I'm sorry. Things— Things are better. Much better."

"AND YOU SAID they're not all hugs and kisses," Eddy said to Ezra, who had shown up at 2:00 p.m. She stood by her oldest brother as they watched their parents, Kennedy and Gerry, Allie Morgan and her husband, and Clark and Berkeley dance to the song. Her father kept singing to her mother.

Gene had vetoed the band, saying he would make a CD for the party.

He had. The CD contained every cover ever recorded of "Let It Be Me."

Ezra said now, deadpan, "I think Julio Iglesias is my favorite."

Eddy snorted. "Why don't you dance with Janina?" Ezra's girlfriend Janina was a departure for him, a vegan yoga teacher and political activist.

Janina, in a silk halter top and floor-length skirt made from a sari, was standing with Gene, listening to him with a somewhat fascinated expression as he told her about the habits of mother scorpions.

Several cousins were down on the dock, drinking beer, and Clark and Berkeley's daughter, Anne, was touring the kennels with a girlfriend.

Bob Dylan's cover started, and Elijah left Sissy and walked over to Gene. "Is there any other music?" he asked.

"It's your song," Gene said matter-of-factly. "I thought it's what you'd want to hear."

Elijah, as had long been his habit with his son, thought carefully before speaking. "Your mother and I thank you for the gift. But I think the other guests might like a change."

Eddy came over and said, "Gene, why don't you tell Dad why you think it's their favorite song. Mom, come here!"

Sissy joined them.

"I don't think it's consciously why," Gene informed Eddy. "Obviously it's a sappy song that was popular when they were teenagers. But unconsciously they like it because it expresses how dogs feel about humans."

Elijah tried hard to keep a straight face. "No matter how little we deserve it."

"It's how I feel about dogs," Sissy said, "but it's even more how I feel about your father."

Gene gave her a look that said this admission was of no interest to him. He turned off the CD player and asked Elijah, "How about the Sex Pistols? I have *Never Mind the Bollocks* in my car."

"Great," said Elijah, deciding not to argue.

Behind him, a cork popped.

While the music paused, Ezra stepped up to the part of the deck where the others had been dancing. He had brought champagne, and now Janina filled glasses.

Finally, when Gene had returned, he said, "To my parents. May the next twenty-five years be even better."

Elijah noticed that he looked uneasily at Clark after he'd made the toast. Clark gave an approving nod.

To my parents, echoed in Elijah's mind. All Ezra's parents.

CHAPTER FIFTEEN

All this, Nick thought, in pursuit of the perfect dog. He wondered what the judge would make of Beezlebub's Herald. Would the offspring of genetically altered dogs beat out old-fashioned organic breeding? Nick admired the sable bitch who'd taken her group in Organic Breeding. Was it his imagination, or was there more happiness, more joy, in this animal?
—*Stud Feats: A Nick D'Angeles Mystery,*
Elijah Workman, 2008

Westminster Kennel Club Dog Show
February 8, 2009

CHAMPION GENESIS'S Let It Be Me was only eleven months old. The sable bitch had earned her championship in the shortest possible time. Sissy personally loved sables, and it surprised and pleased her that Let It Be Me had made it to this show. So many people, judges not excluded, preferred black-and-tans.

"Do you think I should have handled her?" Sissy asked Elijah as they sat together at ringside, watching Berkeley and Mimi in the ring.

"No, Berkeley's the best."

Sissy admired another bitch, older and more solid-looking than Mimi. She chattered mindlessly about other bitches, other handlers. She watched Berkeley gracefully stack Mimi, watched the judge touch the beautiful bitch.

"You know what?" Elijah said.

"What?"

"She's young to be out there, but she's happy. Look how happy she is."

"Yes," Sissy agreed. "She likes Berkeley."

Ezra sat on his father's other side. He said, "The judge likes her."

"Do you think?" Sissy whispered.

They sat, clutching their seats, holding their breath as all the bitches and handlers lined at the end of the ring, awaiting the judge's pick.

He pointed his finger.

Not at Mimi.

Sissy felt tears of disappointment spring to her eyes.

"Mom, you always cry," said Ezra. "My God,

she's at Westminster. She's a puppy! Give her a break."

"I know. She's great," Sissy whispered.

Then she saw the judge hand something to Berkeley. Berkeley looked at it, and a smile broke over her face.

"What's that?" Sissy asked.

"I'm sure he just told her that Mimi's a pretty girl," Ezra said.

They made their way out of their seats to go find Berkeley and Mimi. They met in a corridor off of the ring, and Berkeley held out the piece of paper to Sissy while Mimi promptly jumped up beside Sissy, which was what she did because she wasn't allowed to jump on people. A springing spiral in the air.

Sissy looked at what Berkeley had handed her.

It was an Award of Merit.

The tears came again, but this time they were of joy. She shoved the paper at Elijah and crouched to hug Mimi, who wiggled and kissed her and swished her tail at one beat per half second.

Sissy's cell phone vibrated in her pocket, and as she stood again she took it out. "Hello?"

"Mom, it's Eddy! She looked so pretty. She should have won, but she's just a baby, really."

"She got an Award of Merit. Elijah, you're

crushing me. Your dad's kissing me to death, Eddy."

Sissy made her excuses to Eddy, closed her phone and let herself be enfolded in Elijah's arms.

He said, "You did this, Sissy! You're incredible."

Sissy pulled away enough to look up at him. "We did it, Elijah. We did it."

His eyes on hers, he said steadily, "You're right. We did." He held her tightly, so thankful for the we they were. He kissed her lips softly and said, "There really isn't any you or I anymore, is there?" And this had been his dream of life with her.

She gazed up at him, because what he'd expressed was the long desire of her heart, and it had become true. "Just we," she said, pressing her face against his shoulder in utter contentment.

* * * * *

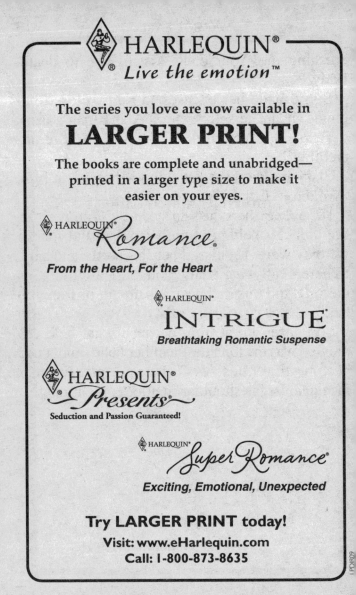

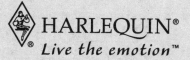

Invites *you* to experience lively, heartwarming all-American romances

Every month, we bring you four strong, sexy men, and four women who know what they want—and go all out to get it.

From small towns to big cities, experience a sense of adventure, romance and family spirit—the all-American way!

Love, Home & Happiness

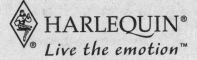

HARLEQUIN®
INTRIGUE®

BREATHTAKING ROMANTIC SUSPENSE

Shared dangers and passions lead to electrifying romance and heart-stopping suspense!

Every month, you'll meet six new heroes who are guaranteed to make your spine tingle and your pulse pound. With them you'll enter into the exciting world of Harlequin Intrigue— where your life is on the line and so is your heart!

THAT'S INTRIGUE—
ROMANTIC SUSPENSE
AT ITS BEST!

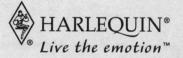

![Harlequin logo] **Harlequin® Historical**
Historical Romantic Adventure!

*Imagine a time of chivalrous
knights and unconventional ladies,
roguish rakes and impetuous
heiresses, rugged cowboys
and spirited frontierswomen—
these rich and vivid tales will
capture your imagination!*

*Harlequin Historical . . .
they're too good to miss!*